BLACKS

BLACKS

GWENDOLYN BROOKS

THIRD WORLD PRESS, CHICAGO, ILLINOIS

Blacks

by Gwendolyn Brooks

Seventh Printing, 1994
Sixth Printing, 1992 Third World Press
Fifth Printing, 1991,Third World Press
Fourth Printing, February 1989
Third Printing, January 1988
Second Printing, September 1987

Some of the material in this compilation has been previously published by Harper and Row, New York, under the following titles: *Maud Martha, The Bean Eaters, In the Mecca, Annie Allen, A Street in Bronzeville* and *The World of Gwendolyn Brooks.*

LCCN: 86-72732
ISBN : 0-88378-1050 (paper)
ISBN: 0-88375-1395 (Cloth)

Gwendolyn Brooks
P.O. Box 19355
Chicago, Illinois 60619

To the Memory
of My Parents,
David and Keziah Brooks

CONTENTS

ACKNOWLEDGMENTS

Annie Allen

The author acknowledges her indebtedness to the John Simon Guggenheim Memorial Foundation of New York.

Some of the poems were published in *Common Ground, Poetry, Negro Story, The Poetry of the Negro,* and *Cross-Section 1945.*

The Bean Eaters

Some of these poems were first published in *Harper's Magazine, Poetry,* and *Voices.*

In the Mecca

Parts of this book were first published in *Negro Digest, Chicago Magazine, Journal of Black Poetry* and *Sisters Today,* and by Broadside Press.

Certain poems in *Beckonings, Riot,* and *Family Pictures* were reprinted in *To Disembark,* and I credit Broadside Press of Detroit and Third World Press of Chicago.

BLACKS

A Street in Bronzeville

1945

A STREET
IN BRONZEVILLE

the old-marrieds

But in the crowding darkness not a word did they say.
Though the pretty-coated birds had piped so lightly all
the day.
And he had seen the lovers in the little side-streets.
And she had heard the morning stories clogged with
sweets.
It was quite a time for loving. It was midnight. It was
May.
But in the crowding darkness not a word did they say.

kitchenette building

We are things of dry hours and the involuntary plan,
Grayed in, and gray. "Dream" makes a giddy sound, not
strong
Like "rent," "feeding a wife," "satisfying a man."

But could a dream send up through onion fumes
Its white and violet, fight with fried potatoes
And yesterday's garbage ripening in the hall,
Flutter, or sing an aria down these rooms

Even if we were willing to let it in,
Had time to warm it, keep it very clean,
Anticipate a message, let it begin?

We wonder. But not well! not for a minute!
Since Number Five is out of the bathroom now,
We think of lukewarm water, hope to get in it.

the mother

ABORTIONS will not let you forget.
You remember the children you got that you did not
get,
The damp small pulps with a little or with no hair,
The singers and workers that never handled the air.
You will never neglect or beat
Them, or silence or buy with a sweet.
You will never wind up the sucking-thumb
Or scuttle off ghosts that come.
You will never leave them, controlling your luscious
sigh,
Return for a snack of them, with gobbling mother-eye.

I have heard in the voices of the wind the voices of my
dim killed children.
I have contracted. I have eased
My dim dears at the breasts they could never suck.
I have said, Sweets, if I sinned, if I seized
Your luck
And your lives from your unfinished reach,
If I stole your births and your names,
Your straight baby tears and your games,
Your stilted or lovely loves, your tumults, your mar-
riages, aches, and your deaths,
If I poisoned the beginnings of your breaths,
Believe that even in my deliberateness I was not de-
liberate.
Though why should I whine,

Whine that the crime was other than mine?—
Since anyhow you are dead.
Or rather, or instead,
You were never made.
But that too, I am afraid,
Is faulty: oh, what shall I say, how is the truth to be
said?
You were born, you had body, you died.
It is just that you never giggled or planned or cried.

Believe me, I loved you all.
Believe me, I knew you, though faintly, and I loved, I
loved you
All.

southeast corner

THE School of Beauty's a tavern now.
The Madam is underground.
Out at Lincoln, among the graves
Her own is early found.
Where the thickest, tallest monument
Cuts grandly into the air
The Madam lies, contentedly.
Her fortune, too, lies there,
Converted into cool hard steel
And right red velvet lining;
While over her tan impassivity
Shot silk is shining.

when Mrs. Martin's Booker T.

WHEN Mrs. Martin's Booker T.
Ruined Rosa Brown
Mrs. Martin moved away
To the low west side of town.
"Don't care if I never see that boy
Again to the end of my days.
He wrung my heart like a chicken neck.
And he made me a disgrace.
Don't come to tell me he's dyin'.
Don't come to tell me he's dead.
But tell me if'n he take that gal
And get her decent wed."

the soft man

DISGUSTING, isn't it, dealing out the damns
To every comer? Hits the heart like pain.
And calling women (Marys) chicks and broads,
Men hep, and cats, or corny to the jive.
Being seen Everywhere (keeping Alive),
Rhumboogie (and the joint is jumpin', Joe),
Brass Rail, Keyhole, De Lisa, Cabin Inn.
And all the other garbage cans.

But grin.
Because there is a clean unanxious place
To which you creep on Sundays. And you cool
In lovely sadness.

No one giggles where
You bathe your sweet vulgarity in prayer.

the funeral

To WHATEVER you incline, your final choice here must
be handling
Occasional sweet clichés with a dishonesty of deft tact.
For these people are stricken, they want none of your
long-range messages,
Only the sweet clichés, to pamper them, modify fright.
Many friends have sent flowers, clubs have been kind
with sprays,
Wreaths. The flowers provide a kind of heat. Sick
Thick odor-loveliness winds nicely about the shape of
mourning,
A dainty horror. People think of flowers upon rot—
And for moments together the corpse is no colder than
they.
They glance at each other, want love from each other:
Or they do not glance but out of tight eyes vaguely pray.

Preacher and tradition of piety and propriety rise. The
people wait
For the dear blindfold: "Heaven is Good denied.
Rich are the men who have died."

hunchback girl: she thinks of heaven

MY FATHER, it is surely a blue place
And straight. Right. Regular. Where I shall find
No need for scholarly nonchalance or looks
A little to the left or guards upon the
Heart to halt love that runs without crookedness
Along its crooked corridors. My Father,
It is a planned place surely. Out of coils,
Unscrewed, released, no more to be marvelous,
I shall walk straightly through most proper halls
Proper myself, princess of properness.

a song in the front yard

I've stayed in the front yard all my life.
I want a peek at the back
Where it's rough and untended and hungry weed grows.
A girl gets sick of a rose.

I want to go in the back yard now
And maybe down the alley,
To where the charity children play.
I want a good time today.

They do some wonderful things.
They have some wonderful fun.
My mother sneers, but I say it's fine
How they don't have to go in at quarter to nine.
My mother, she tells me that Johnnie Mae
Will grow up to be a bad woman.
That George'll be taken to Jail soon or late
(On account of last winter he sold our back gate.)

But I say it's fine. Honest, I do.
And I'd like to be a bad woman, too,
And wear the brave stockings of night-black lace
And strut down the streets with paint on my face.

patent leather

THAT cool chick down on Calumet
Has got herself a brand new cat,
With pretty patent-leather hair.
And he is man enough for her.

Us other guys don't think he's such
A much.
His voice is shrill.
His muscle is pitiful.

That cool chick down on Calumet,
Though, says he's really "it."
And strokes the patent-leather hair
That makes him man enough for her.

the ballad of chocolate Mabbie

IT WAS Mabbie without the grammar school gates.
And Mabbie was all of seven.
And Mabbie was cut from a chocolate bar.
And Mabbie thought life was heaven.

The grammar school gates were the pearly gates,
For Willie Boone went to school.
When she sat by him in history class
Was only her eyes were cool.

It was Mabbie without the grammar school gates
Waiting for Willie Boone.
Half hour after the closing bell!
He would surely be coming soon.

Oh, warm is the waiting for joys, my dears!
And it cannot be too long.
Oh, pity the little poor chocolate lips
That carry the bubble of song!

Out came the saucily bold Willie Boone.
It was woe for our Mabbie now.
He wore like a jewel a lemon-hued lynx
With sand-waves loving her brow.

It was Mabbie alone by the grammar school gates.
Yet chocolate companions had she:
Mabbie on Mabbie with hush in the heart.
Mabbie on Mabbie to be.

the preacher: ruminates behind the sermon

I THINK it must be lonely to be God.
Nobody loves a master. No. Despite
The bright hosannas, bright dear-Lords, and bright
Determined reverence of Sunday eyes.

Picture Jehovah striding through the hall
Of His importance, creatures running out
From servant-corners to acclaim, to shout
Appreciation of His merit's glare.

But who walks with Him?—dares to take His arm,
To slap Him on the shoulder, tweak His ear,
Buy Him a Coca-Cola or a beer,
Pooh-pooh His politics, call Him a fool?

Perhaps—who knows?—He tires of looking down.
Those eyes are never lifted. Never straight.
Perhaps sometimes He tires of being great
In solitude. Without a hand to hold.

Sadie and Maud

MAUD went to college.
Sadie stayed at home.
Sadie scraped life
With a fine-tooth comb.

She didn't leave a tangle in.
Her comb found every strand.
Sadie was one of the livingest chits
In all the land.

Sadie bore two babies
Under her maiden name.
Maud and Ma and Papa
Nearly died of shame.
Every one but Sadie
Nearly died of shame.

When Sadie said her last so-long
Her girls struck out from home.
(Sadie had left as heritage
Her fine-tooth comb.)

Maud, who went to college,
Is a thin brown mouse.
She is living all alone
In this old house.

the independent man

Now who could take you off to tiny life
In one room or in two rooms or in three
And cork you smartly, like the flask of wine
You are? Not any woman. Not a wife.
You'd let her twirl you, give her a good glee
Showing your leaping ruby to a friend.
Though twirling would be meek. Since not a cork
Could you allow, for being made so free.

A woman would be wise to think it well
If once a week you only rang the bell.

obituary for a living lady

My friend was decently wild
As a child.
And as a young girl
She was interested in a brooch and pink powder and a curl.
As a young woman though
She fell in love with a man who didn't know
That even if she wouldn't let him touch her breasts she was still worth his hours,
Stopped calling Sundays with flowers.
Sunday after Sunday she put on her clean, gay (though white) dress,
Worried the windows. There was so much silence she finally decided that the next time she would say "yes."
But the man had found by then a woman who dressed in red.
My friend spent a hundred weeks or so wishing she were dead.
But crying for yourself, when you give it all of your time, gets tedious after a while.
Therefore she terminated her mourning, made for her mouth a sad sweet smile
And discovered the country of God. Now she will not dance
And she thinks not the thinnest thought of any type of romance

And I can't get her to take a touch of the best cream cologne.
However even without lipstick she is lovely and it is no wonder that the preacher (at present) is almost a synonym for her telephone
And watches the neutral kind bland eyes that moisten the first pew center on Sunday—I beg your pardon —Sabbath nights
And wonders as his stomach breaks up into fire and lights
How long it will be
Before he can, with reasonably slight risk of rebuke, put his hand on her knee.

when you have forgotten Sunday: the love story

——And when you have forgotten the bright bedclothes
on a Wednesday and a Saturday,
And most especially when you have forgotten Sunday—
When you have forgotten Sunday halves in bed,
Or me sitting on the front-room radiator in the limping
afternoon
Looking off down the long street
To nowhere,
Hugged by my plain old wrapper of no-expectation
And nothing-I-have-to-do and I'm-happy-why?
And if-Monday-never-had-to-come—
When you have forgotten that, I say,
And how you swore, if somebody beeped the bell,
And how my heart played hopscotch if the telephone
rang;
And how we finally went in to Sunday dinner,
That is to say, went across the front room floor to the
ink-spotted table in the southwest corner
To Sunday dinner, which was always chicken and
noodles
Or chicken and rice
And salad and rye bread and tea
And chocolate chip cookies—
I say, when you have forgotten that,
When you have forgotten my little presentiment
That the war would be over before they got to you;
And how we finally undressed and whipped out the
light and flowed into bed,

And lay loose-limbed for a moment in the week-end
Bright bedclothes,
Then gently folded into each other—
When you have, I say, forgotten all that,
Then you may tell,
Then I may believe
You have forgotten me well.

the murder

THIS is where poor Percy died,
Short of the age of one.
His brother Brucie, with a grin,
Burned him up for fun.

No doubt, poor Percy watched the fire
Chew on his baby dress
With sweet delight, enjoying too
His brother's happiness.

No doubt, poor Percy looked around
And wondered at the heat,
Was worried, wanted Mother,
Who gossiped down the street.

No doubt, poor shrieking Percy died
Loving Brucie still,
Who could, with clean and open eye,
Thoughtfully kill.

Brucie has no playmates now.
His mother mourns his lack.
Brucie keeps on asking, "When
Is Percy comin' back?"

of De Witt Williams on his way to Lincoln Cemetery

He was born in Alabama.
He was bred in Illinois.
He was nothing but a
Plain black boy.

Swing low swing low sweet sweet chariot.
Nothing but a plain black boy.

Drive him past the Pool Hall.
Drive him past the Show.
Blind within his casket,
But maybe he will know.

Down through Forty-seventh Street:
Underneath the L,
And—Northwest Corner, Prairie,
That he loved so well.

Don't forget the Dance Halls—
Warwick and Savoy,
Where he picked his women, where
He drank his liquid joy.

Born in Alabama.
Bred in Illinois.
He was nothing but a
Plain black boy.

Swing low swing low sweet sweet chariot.
Nothing but a plain black boy.

Matthew Cole

HERE are the facts.
He's sixty-six.
He rooms in a stove-heated flat
Over on Lafayette.
He has roomed there ten years long.
He never will be done
With dust and his ceiling that
Is everlasting sad,
And the gloomy housekeeper
Who forgets to build the fire,
And the red fat roaches that stroll
Unafraid up his wall,
And the whiteless grin of the housekeeper
On Saturday night when he pays his four
Dollars, the ceaseless Sunday row
Of her big cheap radio. . . .

She'll tell you he is the pleasantest man—
Always a smile, a smile. . . . But in
The door-locked dirtiness of his room
He never smiles. Except when come,
Say, thoughts of a little boy licorice-full
Without a nickel for Sunday School.
Or thoughts of a little boy playing ball
And swearing at sound of his mother's call.
Once, I think, he laughed aloud,
At thought of a wonderful joke he'd played
On the whole crowd, the old crowd. . . .

the vacant lot

MRS. COLEY'S three-flat brick
Isn't here any more.
All done with seeing her fat little form
Burst out of the basement door;
And with seeing her African son-in-law
(Rightful heir to the throne)
With his great white strong cold squares of teeth
And his little eyes of stone;
And with seeing the squat fat daughter
Letting in the men
When majesty has gone for the day—
And letting them out again.

THE SUNDAYS OF SATIN-LEGS SMITH

INAMORATAS, with an approbation,
Bestowed his title. Blessed his inclination.

He wakes, unwinds, elaborately: a cat
Tawny, reluctant, royal. He is fat
And fine this morning. Definite. Reimbursed.

He waits a moment, he designs his reign,
That no performance may be plain or vain.
Then rises in a clear delirium.

He sheds, with his pajamas, shabby days.
And his desertedness, his intricate fear, the
Postponed resentments and the prim precautions.

Now, at his bath, would you deny him lavender
Or take away the power of his pine?
What smelly substitute, heady as wine,
Would you provide? life must be aromatic.
There must be scent, somehow there must be some.
Would you have flowers in his life? suggest
Asters? a Really Good geranium?
A white carnation? would you prescribe a Show
With the cold lilies, formal chrysanthemum
Magnificence, poinsettias, and emphatic
Red of prize roses? might his happiest
Alternative (you muse) be, after all,

A bit of gentle garden in the best
Of taste and straight tradition? Maybe so.
But you forget, or did you ever know,
His heritage of cabbage and pigtails,
Old intimacy with alleys, garbage pails,
Down in the deep (but always beautiful) South
Where roses blush their blithest (it is said)
And sweet magnolias put Chanel to shame.

No! He has not a flower to his name.
Except a feather one, for his lapel.
Apart from that, if he should think of flowers
It is in terms of dandelions or death.
Ah, there is little hope. You might as well—
Unless you care to set the world a-boil
And do a lot of equalizing things,
Remove a little ermine, say, from kings,
Shake hands with paupers and appoint them men,
For instance—certainly *you* might as well
Leave him his lotion, lavender and oil.

Let us proceed. Let us inspect, together
With his meticulous and serious love,
The innards of this closet. Which is a vault
Whose glory is not diamonds, not pearls,
Not silver plate with just enough dull shine.
But wonder-suits in yellow and in wine,
Sarcastic green and zebra-striped cobalt.
All drapes. With shoulder padding that is wide
And cocky and determined as his pride;
Ballooning pants that taper off to ends

Scheduled to choke precisely.
                                        Here are hats
Like bright umbrellas; and hysterical ties
Like narrow banners for some gathering war.

People are so in need, in need of help.
People want so much that they do not know.

Below the tinkling trade of little coins
The gold impulse not possible to show
Or spend. Promise piled over and betrayed.

These kneaded limbs receive the kiss of silk.
Then they receive the brave and beautiful
Embrace of some of that equivocal wool.
He looks into his mirror, loves himself—
The neat curve here; the angularity
That is appropriate at just its place;
The technique of a variegated grace.

Here is all his sculpture and his art
And all his architectural design.
Perhaps you would prefer to this a fine
Value of marble, complicated stone.
Would have him think with horror of baroque,
Rococo. You forget and you forget.

He dances down the hotel steps that keep
Remnants of last night's high life and distress.
As spat-out purchased kisses and spilled beer.
He swallows sunshine with a secret yelp.

Passes to coffee and a roll or two.
Has breakfasted.
Out. Sounds about him smear,
Become a unit. He hears and does not hear
The alarm clock meddling in somebody's sleep;
Children's governed Sunday happiness;
The dry tone of a plane; a woman's oath;
Consumption's spiritless expectoration;
An indignant robin's resolute donation
Pinching a track through apathy and din;
Restaurant vendors weeping; and the L
That comes on like a slightly horrible thought.

Pictures, too, as usual, are blurred.
He sees and does not see the broken windows
Hiding their shame with newsprint; little girl
With ribbons decking wornness, little boy
Wearing the trousers with the decentest patch,
To honor Sunday; women on their way
From "service," temperate holiness arranged
Ably on asking faces; men estranged
From music and from wonder and from joy
But far familiar with the guiding awe
Of foodlessness.
He loiters.
Restaurant vendors
Weep, or out of them rolls a restless glee.
The Lonesome Blues, the Long-lost Blues, I Want A
Big Fat Mama. Down these sore avenues
Comes no Saint-Saëns, no piquant elusive Grieg,
And not Tschaikovsky's wayward eloquence

And not the shapely tender drift of Brahms.
But could he love them? Since a man must bring
To music what his mother spanked him for
When he was two: bits of forgotten hate,
Devotion: whether or not his mattress hurts:
The little dream his father humored: the thing
His sister did for money: what he ate
For breakfast—and for dinner twenty years
Ago last autumn: all his skipped desserts.

The pasts of his ancestors lean against
Him. Crowd him. Fog out his identity.
Hundreds of hungers mingle with his own,
Hundreds of voices advise so dexterously
He quite considers his reactions his,
Judges he walks most powerfully alone,
That everything is—simply what it is.

But movie-time approaches, time to boo
The hero's kiss, and boo the heroine
Whose ivory and yellow it is sin
For his eye to eat of. The Mickey Mouse,
However, is for everyone in the house.

Squires his lady to dinner at Joe's Eats.
His lady alters as to leg and eye,
Thickness and height, such minor points as these,
From Sunday to Sunday. But no matter what
Her name or body positively she's
In Queen Lace stockings with ambitious heels
That strain to kiss the calves, and vivid shoes

Frontless and backless, Chinese fingernails,
Earrings, three layers of lipstick, intense hat
Dripping with the most voluble of veils.
Her affable extremes are like sweet bombs
About him, whom no middle grace or good
Could gratify. He had no education
In quiet arts of compromise. He would
Not understand your counsels on control, nor
Thank you for your late trouble.

At Joe's Eats

You get your fish or chicken on meat platters.
With coleslaw, macaroni, candied sweets,
Coffee and apple pie. You go out full.
(The end is—isn't it?—all that really matters.)

And even and intrepid come
The tender boots of night to home.

Her body is like new brown bread
Under the Woolworth mignonette.
Her body is a honey bowl
Whose waiting honey is deep and hot.
Her body is like summer earth,
Receptive, soft, and absolute . . .

NEGRO HERO

to suggest Dorie Miller

I HAD to kick their law into their teeth in order to save
them.
However I have heard that sometimes you have to deal
Devilishly with drowning men in order to swim them to
shore.
Or they will haul themselves and you to the trash and
the fish beneath.
(When I think of this, I do not worry about a few
Chipped teeth.)

It is good I gave glory, it is good I put gold on their
name.
Or there would have been spikes in the afterward hands.
But let us speak only of my success and the pictures in
the Caucasian dailies
As well as the Negro weeklies. For I am a gem.
(They are not concerned that it was hardly The Enemy
my fight was against
But them.)

It was a tall time. And of course my blood was
Boiling about in my head and straining and howling
and singing me on.
Of course I was rolled on wheels of my boy itch to get
at the gun.
Of course all the delicate rehearsal shots of my childhood massed in mirage before me.

Of course I was child
And my first swallow of the liquor of battle bleeding
black air dying and demon noise
Made me wild.

It was kinder than that, though, and I showed like a
banner my kindness.
I loved. And a man will guard when he loves.
Their white-gowned democracy was my fair lady.
With her knife lying cold, straight, in the softness of
her sweet-flowing sleeve.
But for the sake of the dear smiling mouth and the
stuttered promise I toyed with my life.
I threw back!—I would not remember
Entirely the knife.

Still—am I good enough to die for them, is my blood
bright enough to be spilled,
Was my constant back-question—are they clear
On this? Or do I intrude even now?
Am I clean enough to kill for them, do they wish me to
kill
For them or is my place while death licks his lips and
strides to them
In the galley still?

(In a southern city a white man said
Indeed, I'd rather be dead;
Indeed, I'd rather be shot in the head
Or ridden to waste on the back of a flood
Than saved by the drop of a black man's blood.)

Naturally, the important thing is, I helped to save them,
them and a part of their democracy.
Even if I had to kick their law into their teeth in order
to do that for them.
And I am feeling well and settled in myself because I
believe it was a good job,
Despite this possible horror: that they might prefer the
Preservation of their law in all its sick dignity and their
knives
To the continuation of their creed
And their lives.

HATTIE SCOTT

the end of the day

It's usually from the insides of the door
That I takes my peek at the sun
Pullin' off his clothes and callin' it a day.
'Cause I'm gettin' the dishes done
About that time. Not that I couldn't
Sneak out on the back porch a bit,
But the sun and me's the same, could be:
Cap the job, then to hell with it.

No lollin' around the old work-place
But off, spite of somethin' to see.
Yes, off, until time when the sun comes back.
Then it's wearily back for me.

the date

IF SHE don't hurry up and let me out of here.
Keeps pilin' up stuff for me to do.
I ain't goin' to finish that ironin'.
She got another think comin'. Hey, you.
Whatcha mean talkin' about cleanin' silver?
It's eight o'clock now, you fool.
I'm leavin'. Got somethin' interestin' on my mind.
Don't mean night school.

at the hairdresser's

GIMME an upsweep, Minnie,
With humpteen baby curls.
'Bout time I got some glamour.
I'll show them girls.

Think they so fly a-struttin'
With they wool a-blowin' 'round.
Wait'll they see my upsweep.
That'll jop 'em back on the ground.

Got Madam C. J. Walker's first.
Got Poro Grower next.
Ain't none of 'em worked with me, Min.
But I ain't vexed.

Long hair's out of style anyhow, ain't it?
Now it's tie it up high with curls.
So gimme an upsweep, Minnie.
I'll show them girls.

when I die

No LODGE with banners flappin'
Will follow after me.
But one lone little short man
Dressed all shabbily.

He'll have his buck-a-dozen,
He'll lay them on with care.
And the angels will be watchin',
And kiss him sweetly there.

Then off he'll take his mournin' black,
And wipe his tears away.
And the girls, they will be waitin'.
There's nothin' more to say.

the battle

MOE BELLE JACKSON'S husband
Whipped her good last night.
Her landlady told my ma they had
A knock-down-drag-out fight.

I like to think
Of how I'd of took a knife
And slashed all of the quickenin'
Out of his lowly life.

But if I know Moe Belle,
Most like, she shed a tear,
And this mornin' it was probably,
"More grits, dear?"

QUEEN OF THE BLUES

MAME was singing
At the Midnight Club.
And the place was red
With blues.
She could shake her body
Across the floor.
For what did she have
To lose?

She put her mama
Under the ground
Two years ago.
(Was it three?)
She covered that grave
With roses and tears.
(A handsome thing
To see.)

She didn't have any
Legal pa
To glare at her,
To shame
Her off the floor
Of the Midnight Club.
Poor Mame.

She didn't have any
Big brother

To shout
"No sister of mine ! . ."
She didn't have any
Small brother
To think she was everything
Fine.

She didn't have any
Baby girl
With velvet
Pop-open eyes.
She didn't have any
Sonny boy
To tell sweet
Sonny boy lies.

"Show me a man
What will love me
Till I die.
Now show me a man
What will love me
Till I die.
Can't find no such a man
No matter how hard
You try.
Go 'long, baby.
Ain't a true man left
In Chi.

"I loved my daddy.
But what did my daddy

Do?
I loved my daddy.
But what did my daddy
Do?
Found him a brown-skin chicken
What's gonna be
Black and blue.

"I was good to my daddy.
Gave him all my dough.
I say, I was good to my daddy.
I gave him all of my dough.
Scrubbed hard in them white folks'
Kitchens
Till my knees was rusty
And so'."

The M.C. hollered,
"Queen of the blues!
Folks, this is strictly
The queen of the blues!"
She snapped her fingers.
She rolled her hips.
What did she have
To lose?

But a thought ran through her
Like a fire.
"Men don't tip their
Hats to me.
They pinch my arms

And they slap my thighs.
But when has a man
Tipped his hat to me?"

Queen of the blues!
Queen of the blues!
Strictly, strictly,
The queen of the blues!

Men are low down
Dirty and mean.
Why don't they tip
Their hats to a queen?

BALLAD OF PEARL MAY LEE

THEN off they took you, off to the jail,
A hundred hooting after.
And you should have heard me at my house.
I cut my lungs with my laughter,
  Laughter,
  Laughter.
I cut my lungs with my laughter.

They dragged you into a dusty cell.
And a rat was in the corner.
And what was I doing? Laughing still.
Though never was a poor gal lorner,
  Lorner,
  Lorner.
Though never was a poor gal lorner.

The sheriff, he peeped in through the bars,
And (the red old thing) he told you,
"You son of a bitch, you're going to hell!"
'Cause you wanted white arms to enfold you,
  Enfold you,
  Enfold you.
'Cause you wanted white arms to enfold you.

But you paid for your white arms, Sammy boy,
And you didn't pay with money.
You paid with your hide and my heart, Sammy boy,
For your taste of pink and white honey,

Honey,
Honey.
For your taste of pink and white honey.

Oh, dig me out of my don't-despair.
Pull me out of my poor-me.
Get me a garment of red to wear.
You had it coming surely,
Surely,
Surely,
You had it coming surely.

At school, your girls were the bright little girls.
You couldn't abide dark meat.
Yellow was for to look at,
Black for the famished to eat.
Yellow was for to look at,
Black for the famished to eat.

You grew up with bright skins on the brain,
And me in your black folks bed.
Often and often you cut me cold,
And often I wished you dead.
Often and often you cut me cold.
Often I wished you dead.

Then a white girl passed you by one day,
And, the vixen, she gave you the wink.
And your stomach got sick and your legs liquefied.
And you thought till you couldn't think.
You thought,

You thought,
You thought till you couldn't think.

I fancy you out on the fringe of town,
The moon an owl's eye minding;
The sweet and thick of the cricket-belled dark,
The fire within you winding . . . .
Winding,
Winding . . . .
The fire within you winding.

Say, she was white like milk, though, wasn't she?
And her breasts were cups of cream.
In the back of her Buick you drank your fill.
Then she roused you out of your dream.
In the back of her Buick you drank your fill.
Then she roused you out of your dream.

"You raped me, nigger," she softly said.
(The shame was threading through.)
"You raped me, nigger, and what the hell
Do you think I'm going to do?
What the hell,
What the hell
Do you think I'm going to do?

"I'll tell every white man in this town.
I'll tell them all of my sorrow.
You got my body tonight, nigger boy.
I'll get your body tomorrow.
Tomorrow.
Tomorrow.
I'll get your body tomorrow."

And my glory but Sammy she did! She did!
And they stole you out of the jail.
They wrapped you around a cottonwood tree.
And they laughed when they heard you wail.
  Laughed,
  Laughed.
They laughed when they heard you wail.

And I was laughing, down at my house.
Laughing fit to kill.
You got what you wanted for dinner,
But brother you paid the bill.
  Brother,
  Brother,
Brother you paid the bill.

You paid for your dinner, Sammy boy,
And you didn't pay with money.
You paid with your hide and my heart, Sammy boy,
For your taste of pink and white honey,
  Honey,
  Honey.
For your taste of pink and white honey.

Oh, dig me out of my don't-despair.
Oh, pull me out of my poor-me.
Oh, get me a garment of red to wear.
You had it coming surely.
  Surely.
  Surely.
You had it coming surely.

GAY CHAPS AT THE BAR

souvenir for Staff Sergeant Raymond Brooks and every other soldier

gay chaps at the bar

. . . and guys I knew in the States, young officers, return from the front crying and trembling. Gay chaps at the bar in Los Angeles, Chicago, New York. . . .

LIEUTENANT WILLIAM COUCH
in the South Pacific

WE KNEW how to order. Just the dash
Necessary. The length of gaiety in good taste.
Whether the raillery should be slightly iced
And given green, or served up hot and lush.
And we knew beautifully how to give to women
The summer spread, the tropics, of our love.
When to persist, or hold a hunger off.
Knew white speech. How to make a look an omen.
But nothing ever taught us to be islands.
And smart, athletic language for this hour
Was not in the curriculum. No stout
Lesson showed how to chat with death. We brought
No brass fortissimo, among our talents,
To holler down the lions in this air.

still do I keep my look, my identity . . .

EACH body has its art, its precious prescribed
Pose, that even in passion's droll contortions, waltzes,
Or push of pain—or when a grief has stabbed,
Or hatred hacked—is its, and nothing else's.
Each body has its pose. No other stock
That is irrevocable, perpetual
And its to keep. In castle or in shack.
With rags or robes. Through good, nothing, or ill.
And even in death a body, like no other
On any hill or plain or crawling cot
Or gentle for the lilyless hasty pall
(Having twisted, gagged, and then sweet-ceased to
    bother),
Shows the old personal art, the look. Shows what
It showed at baseball. What it showed in school.

my dreams, my works, must wait till after hell

I HOLD my honey and I store my bread
In little jars and cabinets of my will.
I label clearly, and each latch and lid
I bid, Be firm till I return from hell.
I am very hungry. I am incomplete.
And none can tell when I may dine again.
No man can give me any word but Wait,
The puny light. I keep eyes pointed in;
Hoping that, when the devil days of my hurt
Drag out to their last dregs and I resume
On such legs as are left me, in such heart
As I can manage, remember to go home,
My taste will not have turned insensitive
To honey and bread old purity could love.

looking

You have no word for soldiers to enjoy
The feel of, as an apple, and to chew
With masculine satisfaction. Not "good-by!"
"Come back!" or "careful!" Look, and let him go.
"Good-by!" is brutal, and "come back!" the raw
Insistence of an idle desperation
Since could he favor he would favor now.
He will be "careful!" if he has permission.
Looking is better. At the dissolution
Grab greatly with the eye, crush in a steel
Of study—Even that is vain. Expression,
The touch or look or word, will little avail,
The brawniest will not beat back the storm
Nor the heaviest haul your little boy from harm.

piano after war

ON A snug evening I shall watch her fingers,
Cleverly ringed, declining to clever pink,
Beg glory from the willing keys. Old hungers
Will break their coffins, rise to eat and thank.
And music, warily, like the golden rose
That sometimes after sunset warms the west,
Will warm that room, persuasively suffuse
That room and me, rejuvenate a past.
But suddenly, across my climbing fever
Of proud delight—a multiplying cry.
A cry of bitter dead men who will never
Attend a gentle maker of musical joy.
Then my thawed eye will go again to ice.
And stone will shove the softness from my face.

mentors

For I am rightful fellow of their band.
My best allegiances are to the dead.
I swear to keep the dead upon my mind,
Disdain for all time to be overglad.
Among spring flowers, under summer trees,
By chilling autumn waters, in the frosts
Of supercilious winter—all my days
I'll have as mentors those reproving ghosts.
And at that cry, at that remotest whisper,
I'll stop my casual business. Leave the banquet.
Or leave the ball—reluctant to unclasp her
Who may be fragrant as the flower she wears,
Make gallant bows and dim excuses, then quit
Light for the midnight that is mine and theirs.

the white troops had their orders but the Negroes looked like men

THEY had supposed their formula was fixed.
They had obeyed instructions to devise
A type of cold, a type of hooded gaze.
But when the Negroes came they were perplexed.
These Negroes looked like men. Besides, it taxed
Time and the temper to remember those
Congenital iniquities that cause
Disfavor of the darkness. Such as boxed
Their feelings properly, complete to tags—
A box for dark men and a box for Other—
Would often find the contents had been scrambled.
Or even switched. Who really gave two figs?
Neither the earth nor heaven ever trembled.
And there was nothing startling in the weather.

firstly inclined to take what it is told

THEE sacrosanct, Thee sweet, Thee crystalline,
With the full jewel wile of mighty light—
With the narcotic milk of peace for men
Who find Thy beautiful center and relate
Thy round command, Thy grand, Thy mystic good—
Thee like the classic quality of a star:
A little way from warmth, a little sad,
Delicately lovely to adore—
I had been brightly ready to believe.
For youth is a frail thing, not unafraid.
Firstly inclined to take what it is told,
Firstly inclined to lean. Greedy to give
Faith tidy and total. To a total God.
With billowing heartiness no whit withheld.

"God works in a mysterious way"

BUT often now the youthful eye cuts down its
Own dainty veiling. Or submits to winds.
And many an eye that all its age had drawn its
Beam from a Book endures the impudence
Of modern glare that never heard of tact
Or timeliness, or Mystery that shrouds
Immortal joy: it merely can direct
Chancing feet across dissembling clods.
Out from Thy shadows, from Thy pleasant meadows,
Quickly, in undiluted light. Be glad, whose
Mansions are bright, to right Thy children's air.
If Thou be more than hate or atmosphere
Step forth in splendor, mortify our wolves.
Or we assume a sovereignty ourselves.

love note
I: surely

SURELY you stay my certain own, you stay
My you. All honest, lofty as a cloud.
Surely I could come now and find you high,
As mine as you ever were; should not be awed.
Surely your word would pop as insolent
As always: "Why, of course I love you, dear."
Your gaze, surely, ungauzed as I could want.
Your touches, that never were careful, what they were.
Surely—But I am very off from that.
From surely. From indeed. From the decent arrow
That was my clean naïveté and my faith.
This morning men deliver wounds and death.
They will deliver death and wounds tomorrow.
And I doubt all. You. Or a violet.

love note
II: flags

STILL, it is dear defiance now to carry
Fair flags of you above my indignation,
Top, with a pretty glory and a merry
Softness, the scattered pound of my cold passion.
I pull you down my foxhole. Do you mind?
You burn in bits of saucy color then.
I let you flutter out against the pained
Volleys. Against my power crumpled and wan.
You, and the yellow pert exuberance
Of dandelion days, unmocking sun;
The blowing of clear wind in your gay hair;
Love changeful in you (like a music, or
Like a sweet mournfulness, or like a dance,
Or like the tender struggle of a fan).

the progress

AND still we wear our uniforms, follow
The cracked cry of the bugles, comb and brush
Our pride and prejudice, doctor the sallow
Initial ardor, wish to keep it fresh.
Still we applaud the President's voice and face.
Still we remark on patriotism, sing,
Salute the flag, thrill heavily, rejoice
For death of men who too saluted, sang.
But inward grows a soberness, an awe,
A fear, a deepening hollow through the cold.
For even if we come out standing up
How shall we smile, congratulate: and how
Settle in chairs? Listen, listen. The step
Of iron feet again. And again wild.

Annie Allen

1949

Memorial to Ed Bland

. . . killed in Germany March 20, 1945;
volunteered for special dangerous mission
. . . wanted to see action . . .

He grew up being curious
And thinking things are various.
Nothing was merely deleterious
Or spurious.

Or good.
His mother could
Not keep him from a popping-eyed surprise
At things. He would
Be digging everywhere, until things gave.
Or did not give. Among his dusty ruins,
Suddenly, there'd be his face to see,
And its queer wonderful expression, salted
With this cool twirling awe.

Yes.
People would see this awe and say they saw
Also what he saw. They could never guess
What they should think. They did what people do:
Smiled out—or frowned.
People like definite decisions,
Tidy answers, all the little ravelings

Snipped off, the lint removed, they
Hop happily among their roughs
Calling what they can't clutch insanity
Or saintliness.

NOTES FROM THE CHILDHOOD AND THE GIRLHOOD

1

the birth in a narrow room

Weeps out of western country something new.
Blurred and stupendous. Wanted and unplanned.
  Winks. Twines, and weakly winks
Upon the milk-glass fruit bowl, iron pot,
The bashful china child tipping forever
Yellow apron and spilling pretty cherries.

Now, weeks and years will go before she thinks
"How pinchy is my room! how can I breathe!
I am not anything and I have got
Not anything, or anything to do!"—
But prances nevertheless with gods and fairies
Blithely about the pump and then beneath
The elms and grapevines, then in darling endeavor
By privy foyer, where the screenings stand
And where the bugs buzz by in private cars
Across old peach cans and old jelly jars.

2
Maxie Allen

Maxie Allen always taught her
Stipendiary little daughter
To thank her Lord and lucky star
For eye that let her see so far,
For throat enabling her to eat
Her Quaker Oats and Cream-of-Wheat,
For tongue to tantrum for the penny,
For ear to hear the haven't-any,
For arm to toss, for leg to chance,
For heart to hanker for romance.

Sweet Annie tried to teach her mother
There was somewhat of something other.
And whether it was veils and God
And whistling ghosts to go unshod
Across the broad and bitter sod,
Or fleet love stopping at her foot
And giving her its never-root
To put into her pocket-book,
Or just a deep and human look,
She did not know; but tried to tell.

Her mother thought at her full well,
In inner voice not like a bell
(Which though not social has a ring
Akin to wrought bedevilling)
But like an oceanic thing:

What do you guess I am?
You've lots of jacks and strawberry jam.
And you don't have to go to bed, I remark,
With two dill pickles in the dark,
Nor prop what hardly calls you honey
And gives you only a little money.

3
the parents: people like our marriage
Maxie and Andrew

Clogged and soft and sloppy eyes
Have lost the light that bites or terrifies.

There are no swans and swallows any more.
The people settled for chicken and shut the door.

But one by one
They got things done:
Watch for porches as you pass
And prim low fencing pinching in the grass.

Pleasant custards sit behind
The white Venetian blind.

4
Sunday chicken

Chicken, she chided early, should not wait
Under the cranberries in after-sermon state.
Who had been beaking about the yard of late.

Elite among the speckle-gray, wild white
On blundering mosaic in the night.
Or lovely baffle-brown. It was not right.

You could not hate the cannibal they wrote
Of, with the nostril bone-thrust, who could dote
On boiled or roasted fellow thigh and throat.

Nor hate the handsome tiger, call him devil
To man-feast, manifesting Sunday evil.

5
old relative

After the baths and bowel-work, he was dead.
Pillows no longer mattered, and getting fed
And anything that anybody said.

Whatever was his he never more strictly had,
Lying in long hesitation. Good or bad,
Hypothesis, traditional and fad.

She went in there to muse on being rid
Of relative beneath the coffin lid.
No one was by. She stuck her tongue out; slid.

Since for a week she must not play "Charmaine"
Or "Honey Bunch," or "Singing in the Rain."

6

downtown vaudeville

What was not pleasant was the hush that coughed
When the Negro clown came on the stage and doffed
His broken hat. The hush, first. Then the soft

Concatenation of delight and lift,
And loud. The decked dismissal of his gift,
The sugared hoot and hauteur. Then, the rift

Where is magnificent, heirloom, and deft
Leer at a Negro to the right, or left—
So joined to personal bleach, and so bereft:

Finding if that is locked, is bowed, or proud.
And what that is at all, spotting the crowd.

7

the ballad of late Annie

Late Annie in her bower lay,
Though sun was up and spinning.
The blush-brown shoulder was so bare,
Blush-brown lip was winning.

Out then shrieked the mother-dear,
"Be I to fetch and carry?
Get a broom to whish the doors
Or get a man to marry."

"Men there were and men there be
But never men so many
Chief enough to marry me,"
Thought the proud late Annie.

"Whom I raise my shades before
Must be gist and lacquer.
With melted opals for my milk,
Pearl-leaf for my cracker."

8
throwing out the flowers

The duck fats rot in the roasting pan,
And it's over and over and all,
The fine fraught smiles, and spites that began
Before it was over and all.

The Thanksgiving praying's away with the silk.
It's over and over and all.
The broccoli, yams and the bead-buttermilk
Are dead with the hail in the hall,
  All
Are dead with the hail in the hall.

The three yellow 'mums and the one white 'mum
Bear to such brusque burial
With pity for little encomium
Since it's over and over and all.

Forgotten and stinking they stick in the can,
And the vase breath's better and all, and all.
And so for the end of our life to a man,
Just over, just over and all.

9
"do not be afraid of no"

"Do not be afraid of no,
Who has so far so very far to go":

New caution to occur
To one whose inner scream set her to cede, for softer lapping and smooth fur!

Whose esoteric need
Was merely to avoid the nettle, to not-bleed.

Stupid, like a street
That beats into a dead end and dies there, with nothing left to reprimand or meet.

And like a candle fixed
Against dismay and countershine of mixed

Wild moon and sun. And like
A flying furniture, or bird with lattice wing; or gaunt thing, a-stammer down a nightmare neon peopled with condor, hawk and shrike.

To say yes is to die
A lot or a little. The dead wear capably their wry

Enameled emblems. They smell.
But that and that they do not altogether yell is all that we know well.

It is brave to be involved,
To be not fearful to be unresolved.

Her new wish was to smile
When answers took no airships, walked a while.

10

"pygmies are pygmies still, though percht on Alps"
—Edward Young

But can see better there, and laughing there
Pity the giants wallowing on the plain.
Giants who bleat and chafe in their small grass,
Seldom to spread the palm; to spit; come clean.

Pygmies expand in cold impossible air,
Cry fie on giantshine, poor glory which
Pounds breast-bone punily, screeches, and has
Reached no Alps: or, knows no Alps to reach.

11
my own sweet good

"Not needing, really, my own sweet good,
To dimple you every day,
For knowing you roam like a gold half-god
And your golden promise was gay.

"Somewhere, you put on your overcoat,
And the others mind what you say
Ill-knowing your route rides to me, roundabout.
For promise so golden and gay.

"Somewhere, you lattice your berries with bran,
Readying for riding my way.
You kiss all the great-lipped girls that you can.
If only they knew that it's little today
And nothing tomorrow to take or to pay,
For sake of a promise so golden, gay,
For promise so golden and gay."

THE ANNIAD

The Anniad

Think of sweet and chocolate,
Left to folly or to fate,
Whom the higher gods forgot,
Whom the lower gods berate;
Physical and underfed
Fancying on the featherbed
What was never and is not.

What is ever and is not.
Pretty tatters blue and red,
Buxom berries beyond rot,
Western clouds and quarter-stars,
Fairy-sweet of old guitars
Littering the little head
Light upon the featherbed.

Think of ripe and rompabout,
All her harvest buttoned in,
All her ornaments untried;
Waiting for the paladin
Prosperous and ocean-eyed
Who shall rub her secrets out
And behold the hinted bride.

Watching for the paladin
Which no woman ever had,
Paradisaical and sad
With a dimple in his chin

And the mountains in the mind;
Ruralist and rather bad,
Cosmopolitan and kind.

Think of thaumaturgic lass
Looking in her looking-glass
At the unembroidered brown;
Printing bastard roses there;
Then emotionally aware
Of the black and boisterous hair,
Taming all that anger down.

And a man of tan engages
For the springtime of her pride,
Eats the green by easy stages,
Nibbles at the root beneath
With intimidating teeth.
But no ravishment enrages.
No dominion is defied.

Narrow master master-calls;
And the godhead glitters now
Cavalierly on his brow.
What a hot theopathy
Roisters through her, gnaws the walls,
And consumes her where she falls
In her gilt humility.

How he postures at his height;
Unfamiliar, to be sure,
With celestial furniture.

Contemplating by cloud-light
His bejewelled diadem;
As for jewels, counting them,
Trying if the pomp be pure.

In the beam his track diffuses
Down her dusted demi-gloom
Like a nun of crimson ruses
She advances. Sovereign
Leaves the heaven she put him in
For the path his pocket chooses;
Leads her to a lowly room.

Which she makes a chapel of.
Where she genuflects to love.
All the prayerbooks in her eyes
Open soft as sacrifice
Or the dolour of a dove.
Tender candles ray by ray
Warm and gratify the gray.

Silver flowers fill the eves
Of the metamorphosis.
And her set excess believes
Incorruptibly that no
Silver has to gape or go,
Deviate to underglow,
Sicken off to hit-or-miss.

Doomer, though, crescendo-comes
Prophesying hecatombs.

Surrealist and cynical.
Garrulous and guttural.
Spits upon the silver leaves.
Denigrates the dainty eves
Dear dexterity achieves.

Names him. Tames him. Takes him off,
Throws to columns row on row.
Where he makes the rifles cough,
Stutter. Where the reveille
Is staccato majesty.
Then to marches. Then to know
The hunched hells across the sea.

Vaunting hands are now devoid.
Hieroglyphics of her eyes
Blink upon a paradise
Paralyzed and paranoid.
But idea and body too
Clamor "Skirmishes can do.
Then he will come back to you."

Less than ruggedly he kindles
Pallors into broken fire.
Hies him home, the bumps and brindles
Of his rummage of desire
Tosses to her lap entire.
Hearing still such eerie stutter.
Caring not if candles gutter.

Tan man twitches: for for long
Life was little as a sand,

Little as an inch of song,
Little as the aching hand
That would fashion mountains, such
Little as a drop from grand
When a heart decides "Too much!"—

Yet there was a drama, drought
Scarleted about the brim
Not with blood alone for him,
Flood, with blossom in between
Retch and wheeling and cold shout,
Suffocation, with a green
Moist sweet breath for mezzanine.

Hometown hums with stoppages.
Now the doughty meanings die
As costumery from streets.
And this white and greater chess
Baffles tan man. Gone the heats
That observe the funny fly
Till the stickum stops the cry.

With his helmet's final doff
Soldier lifts his power off.
Soldier bare and chilly then
Wants his power back again.
No confection languider
Before quick-feast quick-famish Men
Than the candy crowns-that-were.

Hunts a further fervor now.
Shudders for his impotence.

Chases root and vehemence,
Chases stilts and straps to vie
With recession of the sky.
Stiffens: yellows: wonders how
Woman fits for recompense.

Not that woman! (Not that room!
Not that dusted demi-gloom!)
Nothing limpid, nothing meek.
But a gorgeous and gold shriek
With her tongue tucked in her cheek,
Hissing gauzes in her gaze,
Coiling oil upon her ways.

Gets a maple banshee. Gets
A sleek slit-eyed gypsy moan.
Oh those violent vinaigrettes!
Oh bad honey that can hone
Oilily the bluntest stone!
Oh mad bacchanalian lass
That his random passion has!

Think of sweet and chocolate
Minus passing-magistrate,
Minus passing-lofty light,
Minus passing-stars for night,
Sirocco wafts and tra la la,
Minus symbol, cinema
Mirages, all things suave and bright.

Seeks for solaces in snow
In the crusted wintertime.
Icy jewels glint and glow.
Half-blue shadows slanting grow
Over blue and silver rime.
And the crunching in the crust
Chills her nicely, as it must.

Seeks for solaces in green
In the green and fluting spring.
Bubbles apple-green, shrill wine,
Hyacinthine devils sing
In the upper air, unseen
Pucks and cupids make a fine
Fume of fondness and sunshine.

Runs to summer gourmet fare.
Heavy and inert the heat,
Braided round by ropes of scent
With a hypnotist intent.
Think of chocolate and sweet
Wanting richly not to care
That summer hoots at solitaire.

Runs to parks. November leaves
All gone papery and brown
Poise upon the queasy stalks
And perturb the respectable walks.
Glances grayly and perceives
This November her true town:
All's a falling falling down.

Spins, and stretches out to friends.
Cries "I am bedecked with love!"
Cries "I am philanthropist!
Take such rubies as ye list.
Suit to any bonny ends.
Sheathe, expose: but never shove.
Prune, curb, mute: but put above."

Sends down flirting bijouterie.
"Come, oh populace, to me!"
It winks only, and in that light
Are the copies of all her bright
Copies. Glass begets glass. No
Populace goes as they go
Who can need it but at night.

Twists to Plato, Aeschylus,
Seneca and Mimnermus,
Pliny, Dionysius. . . .
Who remove from remarkable hosts
Of agonized and friendly ghosts,
Lean and laugh at one who looks
To find kisses pressed in books.

Tests forbidden taffeta.
Meteors encircle her.
Little lady who lost her twill,
Little lady who lost her fur
Shivers in her thin hurrah,
Pirouettes to pleasant shrill
Appoggiatura with a skill.

But the culprit magics fade.
Stoical the retrograde.
And no music plays at all
In the inner, hasty hall
Which compulsion cut from shade.—
Frees her lover. Drops her hands.
Shorn and taciturn she stands.

Petals at her breast and knee. . . .
"Then incline to children-dear!
Pull the halt magnificence near,
Sniff the perfumes, ribbonize
Gay bouquet most satinly;
Hoard it, for a planned surprise
When the desert terrifies."

Perfumes fly before the gust,
Colors shrivel in the dust,
And the petal velvet shies,
When the desert terrifies:
Howls, revolves, and countercharms:
Shakes its great and gritty arms:
And perplexes with odd eyes.

Hence from scenic bacchanal,
Preshrunk and droll prodigal!
Smallness that you had to spend,
Spent. Wench, whiskey and tail-end
Of your overseas disease
Rot and rout you by degrees.
—Close your fables and fatigues;

Kill that fanged flamingo foam
And the fictive gold that mocks;
Shut your rhetorics in a box;
Pack compunction and go home.
Skeleton, settle, down in bed.
Slide a bone beneath Her head,
Kiss Her eyes so rash and red.

Pursing lips for new good-byeing
Now she folds his rust and cough
In the pity old and staunch.
She remarks his feathers off;
Feathers for such tipsy flying
As this scarcely may re-launch
That is dolesome and is dying.

He leaves bouncy sprouts to store
Caramel dolls a little while,
Then forget him, larger doll
Who would hardly ever loll,
Who would hardly ever smile,
Or bring dill pickles, or core
Fruit, or put salve on a sore.

Leaves his mistress to dismiss
Memories of his kick and kiss,
Grant her lips another smear,
Adjust the posies at her ear,
Quaff an extra pint of beer,
Cross her legs upon the stool,
Slit her eyes and find her fool.

Leaves his devotee to bear
Weight of passing by his chair
And his tavern. Telephone
Hoists her stomach to the air.
Who is starch or who is stone
Washes coffee-cups and hair,
Sweeps, determines what to wear.

In the indignant dark there ride
Roughnesses and spiny things
On infallible hundred heels.
And a bodiless bee stings.
Cyclone concentration reels.
Harried sods dilate, divide,
Suck her sorrowfully inside.

Think of tweaked and twenty-four.
Fuchsias gone or gripped or gray,
All hay-colored that was green.
Soft aesthetic looted, lean.
Crouching low, behind a screen,
Pock-marked eye-light, and the sore
Eaglets of old pride and prey.

Think of almost thoroughly
Derelict and dim and done.
Stroking swallows from the sweat.
Fingering faint violet.
Hugging old and Sunday sun.
Kissing in her kitchenette
The minuets of memory.

Appendix to The Anniad

leaves from a loose-leaf war diary

1

("thousands—killed in action")

You need the untranslatable ice to watch.
You need to loiter a little among the vague
Hushes, the clever evasions of the vagueness
Above the healthy energy of decay.
You need the untranslatable ice to watch,
The purple and black to smell.

Before your horror can be sweet.
Or proper.
Before your grief is other than discreet.

The intellectual damn
Will nurse your half-hurt. Quickly you are well.

But weary. How you yawn, have yet to see
Why nothing exhausts you like this sympathy.

2

The Certainty we two shall meet by God
In a wide Parlor, underneath a Light
Of lights, come Sometime, is no ointment now.
Because we two are worshipers of life,
Being young, being masters of the long-legged stride,
Gypsy arm-swing. We never did learn how
To find white in the Bible. We want nights
Of vague adventure, lips lax wet and warm,
Bees in the stomach, sweat across the brow. Now.

3

the sonnet-ballad

Oh mother, mother, where is happiness?
They took my lover's tallness off to war,
Left me lamenting. Now I cannot guess
What I can use an empty heart-cup for.
He won't be coming back here any more.
Some day the war will end, but, oh, I knew
When he went walking grandly out that door
That my sweet love would have to be untrue.
Would have to be untrue. Would have to court
Coquettish death, whose impudent and strange
Possessive arms and beauty (of a sort)
Can make a hard man hesitate—and change.
And he will be the one to stammer, "Yes."
Oh mother, mother, where is happiness?

THE WOMANHOOD

I

the children of the poor

1

People who have no children can be hard:
Attain a mail of ice and insolence:
Need not pause in the fire, and in no sense
Hesitate in the hurricane to guard.
And when wide world is bitten and bewarred
They perish purely, waving their spirits hence
Without a trace of grace or of offense
To laugh or fail, diffident, wonder-starred.
While through a throttling dark we others hear
The little lifting helplessness, the queer
Whimper-whine; whose unridiculous
Lost softness softly makes a trap for us.
And makes a curse. And makes a sugar of
The malocclusions, the inconditions of love.

2

What shall I give my children? who are poor,
Who are adjudged the leastwise of the land,
Who are my sweetest lepers, who demand
No velvet and no velvety velour;
But who have begged me for a brisk contour,
Crying that they are quasi, contraband
Because unfinished, graven by a hand
Less than angelic, admirable or sure.
My hand is stuffed with mode, design, device.
But I lack access to my proper stone.
And plenitude of plan shall not suffice
Nor grief nor love shall be enough alone
To ratify my little halves who bear
Across an autumn freezing everywhere.

3

And shall I prime my children, pray, to pray?
Mites, come invade most frugal vestibules
Spectered with crusts of penitents' renewals
And all hysterics arrogant for a day.
Instruct yourselves here is no devil to pay.
Children, confine your lights in jellied rules;
Resemble graves; be metaphysical mules;
Learn Lord will not distort nor leave the fray.
Behind the scurryings of your neat motif
I shall wait, if you wish: revise the psalm
If that should frighten you: sew up belief
If that should tear: turn, singularly calm
At forehead and at fingers rather wise,
Holding the bandage ready for your eyes.

4

First fight. Then fiddle. Ply the slipping string
With feathery sorcery; muzzle the note
With hurting love; the music that they wrote
Bewitch, bewilder. Qualify to sing
Threadwise. Devise no salt, no hempen thing
For the dear instrument to bear. Devote
The bow to silks and honey. Be remote
A while from malice and from murdering.
But first to arms, to armor. Carry hate
In front of you and harmony behind.
Be deaf to music and to beauty blind.
Win war. Rise bloody, maybe not too late
For having first to civilize a space
Wherein to play your violin with grace.

5

When my dears die, the festival-colored brightness
That is their motion and mild repartee
Enchanted, a macabre mockery
Charming the rainbow radiance into tightness
And into a remarkable politeness
That is not kind and does not want to be,
May not they in the crisp encounter see
Something to recognize and read as rightness?
I say they may, so granitely discreet,
The little crooked questionings inbound,
Concede themselves on most familiar ground,
Cold an old predicament of the breath:
Adroit, the shapely prefaces complete,
Accept the university of death.

II

Life for my child is simple, and is good.
He knows his wish. Yes, but that is not all.
Because I know mine too.
And we both want joy of undeep and unabiding things,
Like kicking over a chair or throwing blocks out of a window
Or tipping over an ice box pan
Or snatching down curtains or fingering an electric outlet
Or a journey or a friend or an illegal kiss.
No. There is more to it than that.
It is that he has never been afraid.
Rather, he reaches out and lo the chair falls with a beautiful crash,
And the blocks fall, down on the people's heads,
And the water comes slooshing sloppily out across the floor.
And so forth.
Not that success, for him, is sure, infallible.
But never has he been afraid to reach.
His lesions are legion.
But reaching is his rule.

III

the ballad of the light-eyed little girl

Sweet Sally took a cardboard box,
And in went pigeon poor.
Whom she had starved to death but not
For lack of love, be sure.

The wind it harped as twenty men.
The wind it harped like hate.
It whipped our light-eyed little girl,
It made her wince and wait.

It screeched a hundred elegies
As it punished her light eyes
(Though only kindness covered these)
And it made her eyebrows rise.

"Now bury your bird," the wind it bawled,
"And bury him down and down
Who had to put his trust in one
So light-eyed and so brown.

"So light-eyed and so villainous,
Who whooped and who could hum
But could not find the time to toss
Confederate his crumb."

She has taken her passive pigeon poor,
She has buried him down and down.

He never shall sally to Sally
Nor soil any roofs of the town.

She has sprinkled nail polish on dead dandelions.
And children have gathered around
Funeral for him whose epitaph
Is "PIGEON—Under the ground."

IV

A light and diplomatic bird
Is lenient in my window tree.
A quick dilemma of the leaves
Discloses twist and tact to me.

Who strangles his extremest need
For pity of my imminence
On utmost ache and lacquered cold
Is prosperous in proper sense:

He can abash his barmecides;
The fantoccini of his range
Pass over. Vast and secular
And apt and admirably strange.

Augmented by incorrigible
Conviction of his symmetry,
He can afford his sine die.
He can afford to pity me

Whose hours at best are wheats or beiges
Lashed with riot-red and black.
Tabasco at the lapping wave.
Search-light in the secret crack.

Oh open, apostolic height!
And tell my humbug how to start
Bird balance, bleach: make miniature
Valhalla of my heart.

V

old laughter

The men and women long ago
In Africa, in Africa,
Knew all there was of joy to know.
In sunny Africa
The spices flew from tree to tree.
The spices trifled in the air
That carelessly
Fondled the twisted hair.

The men and women richly sang
In land of gold and green and red.
The bells of merriment richly rang.

But richness is long dead,
Old laughter chilled, old music done
In bright, bewildered Africa.

The bamboo and the cinnamon
Are sad in Africa.

VI

the rites for Cousin Vit

Carried her unprotesting out the door.
Kicked back the casket-stand. But it can't hold her,
That stuff and satin aiming to enfold her,
The lid's contrition nor the bolts before.
Oh oh. Too much. Too much. Even now, surmise,
She rises in the sunshine. There she goes,
Back to the bars she knew and the repose
In love-rooms and the things in people's eyes.
Too vital and too squeaking. Must emerge.
Even now she does the snake-hips with a hiss,
Slops the bad wine across her shantung, talks
Of pregnancy, guitars and bridgework, walks
In parks or alleys, comes haply on the verge
Of happiness, haply hysterics. Is.

VII
I love those little booths at Benvenuti's

They get to Benvenuti's. There are booths
To hide in while observing tropical truths
About this—dusky folk, so clamorous!
So colorfully incorrect,
So amorous,
So flatly brave!
Boothed-in, one can detect,
Dissect.

One knows and scarcely knows what to expect.

What antics, knives, what lurching dirt; what ditty—
Dirty, rich, carmine, hot, not bottled up,
Straining in sexual soprano, cut
And praying in the bass, partial, unpretty.

They sit, sup,
(Whose friends, if not themselves, arrange
To rent in Venice "a very large cabana,
Small palace," and eat mostly what is strange.)
They sit, they settle; presently are met
By the light heat, the lazy upward whine
And lazy croaky downward drawl of "Tanya."
And their interiors sweat.
They lean back in the half-light, stab their stares
At: walls, panels of imitation oak
With would-be marbly look; linoleum squares

Of dusty rose and brown with little white splashes,
White curls; a vendor tidily encased;
Young yellow waiter moving with straight haste,
Old oaken waiter, lolling and amused;
Some paper napkins in a water glass;
Table, initialed, rubbed, as a desk in school.

They stare. They tire. They feel refused,
Feel overwhelmed by subtle treasons!
Nobody here will take the part of jester.

The absolute stutters, and the rationale
Stoops off in astonishment.
But not gaily
And not with their consent.

They play "They All Say I'm The Biggest Fool"
And "Voo Me On The Vot Nay" and "New Lester
Leaps In" and "For Sentimental Reasons."

But how shall they tell people they have been
Out Bronzeville way? For all the nickels in
Have not bought savagery or defined a "folk."

The colored people will not "clown."

The colored people arrive, sit firmly down,
Eat their Express Spaghetti, their T-bone steak,
Handling their steel and crockery with no clatter,
Laugh punily, rise, go firmly out of the door.

VIII

Beverly Hills, Chicago

("and the people live till they have white hair")

E. M. Price

The dry brown coughing beneath their feet,
(Only a while, for the handyman is on his way)
These people walk their golden gardens.
We say ourselves fortunate to be driving by today.

That we may look at them, in their gardens where
The summer ripeness rots. But not raggedly.
Even the leaves fall down in lovelier patterns here.
And the refuse, the refuse is a neat brilliancy.

When they flow sweetly into their houses
With softness and slowness touched by that everlasting
gold,
We know what they go to. To tea. But that does not mean
They will throw some little black dots into some water and
add sugar and the juice of the cheapest lemons that
are sold,

While downstairs that woman's vague phonograph bleats,
"Knock me a kiss."
And the living all to be made again in the sweatingest
physical manner
Tomorrow. . . . Not that anybody is saying that these people
have no trouble.
Merely that it is trouble with a gold-flecked beautiful
banner.

Nobody is saying that these people do not ultimately cease
to be. And
Sometimes their passings are even more painful than ours.
It is just that so often they live till their hair is white.
They make excellent corpses, among the expensive
flowers. . . .

Nobody is furious. Nobody hates these people.
At least, nobody driving by in this car.
It is only natural, however, that it should occur to us
How much more fortunate they are than we are.

It is only natural that we should look and look
At their wood and brick and stone
And think, while a breath of pine blows,
How different these are from our own.

We do not want them to have less.
But it is only natural that we should think we have not
enough.
We drive on, we drive on.
When we speak to each other our voices are a little gruff.

IX
truth

And if sun comes
How shall we greet him?
Shall we not dread him,
Shall we not fear him
After so lengthy a
Session with shade?

Though we have wept for him,
Though we have prayed
All through the night-years—
What if we wake one shimmering morning to
Hear the fierce hammering
Of his firm knuckles
Hard on the door?

Shall we not shudder?—
Shall we not flee
Into the shelter, the dear thick shelter
Of the familiar
Propitious haze?

Sweet is it, sweet is it
To sleep in the coolness
Of snug unawareness.

The dark hangs heavily
Over the eyes.

X

Exhaust the little moment. Soon it dies.
And be it gash or gold it will not come
Again in this identical disguise.

XI

One wants a Teller in a time like this.

One's not a man, one's not a woman grown,
To bear enormous business all alone.

One cannot walk this winding street with pride,
Straight-shouldered, tranquil-eyed,
Knowing one knows for sure the way back home.
One wonders if one has a home.

One is not certain if or why or how.
One wants a Teller now:—

Put on your rubbers and you won't catch cold.
Here's hell, there's heaven. Go to Sunday School.
Be patient, time brings all good things—(and cool
Strong balm to calm the burning at the brain?)—
Behold,
Love's true, and triumphs; and God's actual.

XII
beauty shoppe

facial

"We use Ardena here." Madame Celeste
Herself in charge, with hot tough-handed licks
To tighten contours (Nature wearying)
Or to release a ropy ruggedness.
Her stomach sitting softly on her lap,
Our Mrs. Breck awaits the miracle.
Pimples must mash themselves in, blotches fade,
Crepe shudder out to satin. Nothing less.
Only a facial. But won't she withdraw
In Beauty, her two centuries of pounds
Shucked to a sweet one-fifty, little eyes
Enormous, lit, and dewy as a doe's?
Madame Celeste works with a wordless haste.
And in an hour our big bird's fixed and flown,
Having paid for what she wants to be. Guilty
With invisible Beauty, up the street she goes.

manicure

He's betting on it this yellow mellow bit
Is buyable. Regal or Met, he'd say,
A Gordon's Dry at the Tavern. And she's got.
Her signals call. The undernourished brows.
The red fat smudge that won't make up its mind
Whether to nip nose, chin, or both together.

The face snowed under. The irresolute modesty.
Those eyes—Mayhap this chick is on the House!
To the approach. Outrageous? guy-gallant?
Paternal? frosty-with-the-heart-of-fire?
Already, this hors-d'oeuvre is in the teeth,
And all a brother has to do is bite.
Ready! . . . Aim! . . . Fire! The glass eyes break. The red
Fat moves and melts. Brows rise in lean surprise.
Bosom awakes. Maybe, she says. She might.
Well, possibly. . . . Well, call at nine tonight.

shampoo-press-hot-oil-&-croquignole
(the smoking iron)

Lay it on lightly, lay it on with heed.
Because it took that stuff so long to grow.

XIII
intermission

1
(deep summer)

By all things planetary, sweet, I swear
Those hands may not possess these hands again
Until I get me gloves of ice to wear.
Because you are the headiest of men!
Your speech is whiskey, and your grin is gin.
I am well drunken. Is there water near?
I've need of wintry air to crisp me in.
—But come here—let me put this in your ear:
I would not want them now! You gave me this
Wildness to gulp. Now water is too pale.
And now I know deep summer is a bliss
I have no wish for weathering the gale.
So when I beg for gloves of ice to wear,
Laugh at me. I am lying, sweet, I swear!

2

High up he hoisted me, and cruel rock
Was lovely for a love seat. Then our talk
Came, making sweet-mouth waves ridiculous,
Who could not hope to honey it with us.

High up he hoisted me, after the year.
And rock was silly business for a chair.
We tried to make the waves ridiculous.
But sweet-mouth waves got very square with us.

3

Stand off, daughter of the dusk,
And do not wince when the bronzy lads
Hurry to cream-yellow shining.
It is plausible. The sun is a lode.

True, there is silver under
The veils of the darkness.
But few care to dig in the night
For the possible treasure of stars.

XIV

People protest in sprawling lightless ways
Against their deceivers, they are never meek—
Conceive their furies, and abort them early;
Are hurt, and shout, weep without form, are surly;
Or laugh, but save their censures and their damns.

And ever complex, ever taut, intense,
You hear man crying up to Any one—
"Be my reviver; be my influence,
My reinstated stimulus, my loyal.
Enable me to give my golds goldly.
To win.
To
Take out a skulk, to put a fortitude in.
Give me my life again, whose right is quite
The charm of porcelain, the vigor of stone."

And he will follow many a cloven foot.

XV

Men of careful turns, haters of forks in the road,
The strain at the eye, that puzzlement, that awe—
Grant me that I am human, that I hurt,
That I can cry.

Not that I now ask alms, in shame gone hollow,
Nor cringe outside the loud and sumptuous gate.
Admit me to our mutual estate.

Open my rooms, let in the light and air.
Reserve my service at the human feast.
And let the joy continue. Do not hoard silence
For the moment when I enter, tardily,
To enjoy my height among you. And to love you
No more as a woman loves a drunken mate,
Restraining full caress and good My Dear,
Even pity for the heaviness and the need—
Fearing sudden fire out of the uncaring mouth,
Boiling in the slack eyes, and the traditional blow.
Next, the indifference formal, deep and slow.

Comes in your graceful glider and benign,
To smile upon me bigly; now desires
Me easy, easy; claims the days are softer
Than they were; murmurs reflectively "Remember
When cruelty, metal, public, uncomplex,
Trampled you obviously and every hour. . . ."
(Now cruelty flaunts diplomas, is elite,

Delicate, has polish, knows how to be discreet):
    Requests my patience, wills me to be calm,
    Brings me a chair, but the one with broken straw,
    Whispers "My friend, no thing is without flaw.
    If prejudice is native—and it is—you
    Will find it ineradicable—not to
    Be juggled, not to be altered at all,
    But left unvexed at its place in the properness
    Of things, even to be given (with grudging) honor.
        What
    We are to hope is that intelligence
    Can sugar up our prejudice with politeness.
    Politeness will take care of what needs caring.
    For the line is there.
    And has a meaning. So our fathers said—
    And they were wise—we think—At any rate,
    They were older than ourselves. And the report is
    What's old is wise. At any rate, the line is
    Long and electric. Lean beyond and nod.
    Be sprightly. Wave. Extend your hand and teeth.
    But never forget it stretches there beneath."
The toys are all grotesque
And not for lovely hands; are dangerous,
Serrate in open and artful places. Rise.
Let us combine. There are no magics or elves
Or timely godmothers to guide us. We are lost, must
Wizard a track through our own screaming weed.

Maud Martha

1953

1

description of Maud Martha

WHAT she liked was candy buttons, and books, and painted music (deep blue, or delicate silver) and the west sky, so altering, viewed from the steps of the back porch; and dandelions.

She would have liked a lotus, or China asters or the Japanese Iris, or meadow lilies—yes, she would have liked meadow lilies, because the very word meadow made her breathe more deeply, and either fling her arms or want to fling her arms, depending on who was by, rapturously up to whatever was watching in the sky. But dandelions were what she chiefly saw. Yellow jewels for everyday, studding the patched green dress of her back yard. She liked their demure prettiness second to their everydayness; for in that latter quality she thought she saw a picture of herself, and it was comforting to find that what was common could also be a flower.

And could be cherished! To be cherished was the dearest wish of the heart of Maud Martha Brown, and sometimes when she was not looking at dandelions (for one would not be looking at them all the time, often there were chairs and tables to dust or tomatoes to slice or beds to make or grocery stores to be gone to, and in the colder months there were no dandelions at all), it was hard to believe that a thing of only ordinary allurements—if the allurements of any flower could be said to be ordinary—was as easy to love as a thing of heart-catching beauty.

Such as her sister Helen! who was only two years past her own age of seven, and was almost her own height and weight and thickness. But oh, the long lashes, the grace, the little ways with the hands and feet.

2

spring landscape: detail

THE school looked solid. Brownish-red brick, dirty cream stone trim. Massive chimney, candid, serious. The sky was gray, but the sun was making little silver promises somewhere up there, hinting. A wind blew. What sort of June day was this? It was more like the last days of November. It was more than rather bleak; still, there were these little promises, just under cover; whether they would fulfill themselves was anybody's guess.

spring landscape: detail

Up the street, mixed in the wind, blew the children, and turned the corner onto the brownish-red brick school court. It was wonderful. Bits of pink, of blue, white, yellow, green, purple, brown, black, carried by jerky little stems of brown or yellow or brown-black, blew by the unhandsome gray and decay of the double-apartment buildings, past the little plots of dirt and scanty grass that held up their narrow brave banners: PLEASE KEEP OFF THE GRASS—NEWLY SEEDED. There were lives in the buildings. Past the tiny lives the children blew. Cramp, inhibition, choke—they did not trouble themselves about these. They spoke shrilly of ways to fix curls and pompadours, of "nasty" boys and "sharp" boys, of Joe Louis, of ice cream, of bicycles, of baseball, of teachers, of examinations, of Duke Ellington, of Bette Davis. They spoke—or at least Maud Martha spoke—of the sweet potato pie that would be served at home.

It was six minutes to nine; in one minute the last bell would ring. "Come on! You'll be late!" Low cries. A quickening of steps. A fluttering of brief cases. Inevitably, though, the fat girl, who was forced to be nonchalant, who pretended she little cared whether she was late or not, who would *not* run! (Because she would wobble, would lose her dignity.) And inevitably the little fellows in knickers, ten, twelve, thirteen years old, nonchalant just for the fun of it—who lingered on the red bricks, throwing balls to each other, or reading newspapers and comic books, or punching each other half playfully.

But eventually every bit of the wind managed to blow itself in, and by five minutes after nine the school court was bare. There was not a hot cap nor a bow ribbon anywhere.

3

love and gorillas

so the gorilla really did escape!

She was sure of it, now that she was awake. For she was awake. This was awakeness. Stretching, curling her fingers, she was still rather protected by the twists of thin smoky stuff from the too sudden onslaught of the red draperies with white and green flowers on them, and the picture of the mother and dog loving a baby, and the dresser with blue paper flowers on it. But that she was now awake in all earnest she could not doubt.

That train—a sort of double-deck bus affair, traveling in a blue-lined half dark. Slow, that traveling. Slow. More like a boat. It came to a stop before the gorilla's cage. The gorilla, lying back, his arms under his head, one leg resting casually across the other, watched the people. Then he rose, lumbered over to the door of his cage, peered, clawed at his bars, shook his bars. All the people on the lower deck climbed to the upper deck.

But why would they not get off?

"Motor trouble!" called the conductor. "Motor trouble! And the gorilla, they think, will escape!"

But why would not the people get off?

Then there was flaring green and there was red and there was red-orange, and she was in the middle of it, her few years many times added to, doubtless, for she was treated as an adult. All the people were afraid, but no one would get off.

All the people wondered if the gorilla would escape.

Awake, she knew he had.

love and gorillas

She was safe, but the others—were they eaten? and if so had he begun on the heads first? and could he eat such things as buttons and watches and hair? or would he first tear those away?

Maud Martha got up, and on her way to the bathroom cast a glance toward her parents' partly open door. Her parents were close together. Her father's arm was around her mother.

Why, how lovely!

For she remembered last night. Her father stamping out grandly, dressed in his nicest suit and hat, and her mother left alone. Later, she and Helen and Harry had gone out with their mother for a "night hike."

How she loved a "hike." Especially in the evening, for then everything was moody, odd, deliciously threatening, always hunched and ready to close in on you but never doing so. East of Cottage Grove you saw fewer people, and those you did see had, all of them (how strange, thought Maud Martha), white faces. Over there that matter of mystery and hunchedness was thicker, a hundred-fold.

Shortly after they had come in, Daddy had too. The children had been sent to bed, and off Maud Martha had gone to her sleep and her gorilla. (Although she had not known that in the beginning, oh no!) In the deep deep night she had waked, just a little, and had called "Mama." Mama had said, "Shut up!"

The little girl did not mind being told harshly to shut up when her mother wanted it quiet so that she and Daddy could love each other.

Because she was very *very* happy that their quarrel was over and that they would once again be nice.

Even though while the loud hate or silent cold was going on, Mama was so terribly sweet and good to her.

4

death of Grandmother

THEY had to sit in a small lobby, waiting for the nurses to change Gramma.

"She can't control herself," explained Maud Martha's mother.

Oh what a thing! What a thing.

When finally they could be admitted, Belva Brown, Maud Martha and Harry tiptoed into the lackluster room, single file.

Gramma lay in what seemed to Maud Martha a wooden coffin. Boards had been put up on either side of the bed to keep the patient from harming herself. All the morning, a nurse confided, Ernestine Brown had been trying to get out of the bed and go home.

They looked in the coffin. Maud Martha felt sick. That was not her Gramma. Couldn't be. Elongated, pulpy-looking face. Closed eyes; lashes damp-appearing, heavy lids. Straight flat thin form under a dark gray blanket. And the voice thick and raw. "Hawh—hawh—hawh." Maud Martha was frightened. But she mustn't show it. She spoke to the semi-corpse.

"Hello, Gramma. This is Maudie." After a moment, "Do you know me, Gramma?"

"Hawh—"

"Do you feel better? Does anything hurt you?"

"Hawh—" Here Gramma slightly shook her head. She did not open her eyes, but apparently she could understand whatever they said. And maybe, thought Maud Martha, what we are not saying.

How alone they were, how removed from this

woman, this ordinary woman who had suddenly become a queen, for whom presently the most interesting door of them all would open, who, lying locked in boards with her "hawhs," yet towered, triumphed over them, while they stood there asking the stupid questions people ask the sick, out of awe, out of half horror, half envy.

"I never saw anybody die before," thought Maud Martha. "But I'm seeing somebody die now."

What was that smell? When would her mother go? She could not stand much more. What was that smell? She turned her gaze away for a while. To look at the other patients in the room, instead of at Gramma! The others were white women. There were three of them, two wizened ones, who were asleep, a stout woman of about sixty, who looked insane, and who was sitting up in bed, wailing, "Why don't they come and bring me a bedpan? Why don't they? Nobody brings me a bedpan." She clutched Maud Martha's coat hem, and stared up at her with glass-bright blue eyes, begging, "Will you tell them to bring me a bedpan? Will you?" Maud Martha promised, and the weak hand dropped.

"Poor dear," said the stout woman, glancing tenderly at Gramma.

When they finally left the room and the last "hawh," Maud Martha told a nurse passing down the hall just then about the woman who wanted the bedpan. The nurse tightened her lips. "Well, she can keep on wanting," she said, after a moment's indignant silence. "That's all they do, day long, night long—whine for the bedpan. We can't give them the bedpan every two minutes. Just forget it, Miss."

They started back down the long corridor. Maud Martha put her arm around her mother.

"Oh Mama," she whimpered, "she—she looked awful. I had no idea. I never saw such a horrible—creature—" A hard time she had, keeping the tears back. And as for her brother, Harry had not said a word since entering the hospital.

When they got back to the house, Papa was receiving a telephone message. Ernestine Brown was dead.

She who had taken the children of Abraham Brown to the circus, and who had bought them pink popcorn, and Peanut Crinkle candy, who had laughed—that Ernestine was dead.

5

you're being so good, so kind

MAUD MARTHA looked the living room over. Nicked old upright piano. Sag-seat leather armchair. Three or four straight chairs that had long ago given up the ghost of whatever shallow dignity they may have had in the beginning and looked completely disgusted with themselves and with the Brown family. Mantel with scroll decorations that usually seemed rather elegant but which since morning had become unspeakably vulgar, impossible.

There was a small hole in the sad-colored rug, near the sofa. Not an outrageous hole. But she shuddered. She dashed to the sofa, maneuvered it till the hole could not be seen.

She sniffed a couple of times. Often it was said that colored people's houses necessarily had a certain heavy, unpleasant smell. Nonsense, that was. Vicious—and nonsense. But she raised every window.

Here was the theory of racial equality about to be put into practice, and she only hoped she would be equal to being equal.

No matter how taut the terror, the fall proceeds to its dregs. . . .

At seven o'clock her heart was starting to make itself heard, and with great energy she was assuring herself that, though she liked Charles, though she admired Charles, it was only at the high school that she wanted to see Charles.

This was no Willie or Richard or Sylvester coming to call on her. Neither was she Charles's Sally or Joan. She was the whole "colored" race, and

Charles was the personalization of the entire Caucasian plan.

At three minutes to eight the bell rang, hesitantly. Charles! No doubt regretting his impulse already. No doubt regarding, with a rueful contempt, the outside of the house, so badly in need of paint. Those rickety steps. She retired into the bathroom. Presently she heard her father go to the door; her father—walking slowly, walking patiently, walking unafraid, as if about to let in a paper boy who wanted his twenty cents, or an insurance man, or Aunt Vivian, or no more than Woodette Williams, her own silly friend.

What was this she was feeling now? Not fear, not fear. A sort of gratitude! It sickened her to realize it. As though Charles, in coming, gave her a gift.

Recipient and benefactor.

It's so good of you.

You're being so good.

6

at the Regal

THE applause was quick. And the silence—final.

That was what Maud Martha, sixteen and very erect, believed, as she manipulated herself through a heavy outflowing crowd in the lobby of the Regal Theatre on Forty-seventh and South Park.

She thought of fame, and of that singer, that Howie Joe Jones, that tall oily brown thing with hair set in thickly pomaded waves, with cocky teeth, eyes like thin glass. With—a Voice. A Voice that Howie Joe's publicity described as "rugged honey." She had not been favorably impressed. She had not been able to thrill. Not even when he threw his head back so that his waves dropped low, shut his eyes sweetly, writhed, thrust out his arms (really *gave* them to the world) and thundered out, with passionate seriousness, with deep meaning, with high purpose—

—Sa-WEET sa-OOOO
Jaust-a YOOOOOOO—

Maud Martha's brow wrinkled. The audience had applauded. Had stamped its strange, hilarious foot. Had put its fingers in its mouth—whistled. Had sped a shininess up to its eyes. But now part of it was going home, as she was, and its face was dull again. It had not been helped. Not truly. Not well. For a hot half hour it had put that light gauze across its little miseries and monotonies, but now here they were again, ungauzed, self-assertive, cancerous as ever. The audience had gotten a fairy gold. And it was not going to spend the rest of its life, or even the rest of the night, being grateful to Howie Joe Jones. No, it would not make plans to raise a hard monument to him.

She swung out of the lobby, turned north.

The applause was quick.

But the silence was final, so what was the singer's profit?

Money.

You had to admit Howie Joe Jones was making money. Money that was raced to the track, to the De Lisa, to women, to the sellers of cars; to Capper and Capper, to Henry C. Lytton and Company for those suits in which he looked like an upright corpse. She read all about it in the columns of the Chicago *Defender's* gossip departments.

She had never understood how people could parade themselves on a stage like that, exhibit their precious private identities; shake themselves about; be very foolish for a thousand eyes.

She was going to keep herself to herself. She did not want fame. She did not want to be a "star."

To create—a role, a poem, picture, music, a rapture in stone: great. But not for her.

What she wanted was to donate to the world a good Maud Martha. That was the offering, the bit of art, that could not come from any other.

She would polish and hone that.

7

Tim

OH, how he used to wriggle!—do little mean things! do great big wonderful things! and laugh laugh laugh.

He had shaved and he had scratched himself through the pants. He had lain down and ached for want of a woman. He had married. He had wiped out his nostrils with bits of tissue paper in the presence of his wife and his wife had turned her head, quickly, but politely, to avoid seeing them as they dropped softly into the toilet, and floated. He had had a big stomach and an alarmingly loud laugh. He had been easy with the ain'ts and sho-nuffs. He had been drunk one time, only one time, and on that occasion had done the Charleston in the middle of what was then Grand Boulevard and is now South Park, at four in the morning. Here was a man who had absorbed the headlines in the *Tribune,* studied the cartoons in *Collier's* and the *Saturday Evening Post.*

These facts she had known about her Uncle Tim. And she had known that he liked sweet potato pie. But what were the facts that she had not known, that his wife, her father's sister Nannie, had not known? The things that nobody had known.

Maud Martha looked down at the gray clay lying hard-lipped, cold, definitely not about to rise and punch off any alarm clock, on the tufted white satin that was at once so beautiful and so ghastly. I must tell them, she thought, as she walked back to her seat, I must let Helen and Harry know how

I want to be arranged in my casket; I don't want my head straight up like that; I want my head turned a little to the right, so my best profile will be showing; and I want my left hand resting on my breast, nicely; and I want my hair plain, not waved—I don't want to look like a gray clay doll.

It all came down to gray clay.

Then just what was important? What had been important about this life, this Uncle Tim? Was the world any better off for his having lived? A little, perhaps. Perhaps he had stopped his car short once, and saved a dog, so that another car could kill it a month later. Perhaps he had given some little street wretch a nickel's worth of peanuts in its unhappy hour, and that little wretch would grow up and forget Uncle Tim but all its life would carry in its heart an anonymous, seemingly underivative softness for mankind. Perhaps. Certainly he had been good to his wife Nannie. She had never said a word against him.

But how important was this, what was the real importance of this, what would—God say? Oh, no! What she would rather mean was, what would Uncle Tim say, if he could get back?

Maud Martha looked at Aunt Nannie. Aunt Nannie had put too much white powder on her face. Was it irreverent, Maud Martha wondered, to be able to think of powdering your face for a funeral, when you were the new widow? Not in this case, she decided, for (she remembered this other thing about him) Uncle Tim, whose nose was always oily, had disliked an oily nose. Aunt Nannie was being brave. As yet she had not dropped a tear. But then, her turn at the casket had not come.

A large woman in a white uniform and white stockings and low-heeled white shoes was playing "We Shall Understand It Better By and By" at the organ, almost inaudibly (with a little jazz roll in her bass). How gentle the music was, how suggestive. Maud Martha saw people, after having all but knocked themselves out below, climbing up the golden, golden stairs, to a throne where sat Jesus, or the Almighty God; who promptly opened a

Book, similar to the arithmetic book she had had in grammar school, turned to the back, and pointed out—the Answers! And the people, poor little things, nodding and cackling among themselves—"So that was it all the time! that is what I should have done!" "But—so simple! so *easy!* I should just have turned here! instead of there!" How wonderful! Was it true? Were people to get the Answers in the sky? Were people really going to understand It better by and by? When it was too late?

8

home

WHAT had been wanted was this always, this always to last, the talking softly on this porch, with the snake plant in the jardiniere in the southwest corner, and the obstinate slip from Aunt Eppie's magnificent Michigan fern at the left side of the friendly door. Mama, Maud Martha and Helen rocked slowly in their rocking chairs, and looked at the late afternoon light on the lawn, and at the emphatic iron of the fence and at the poplar tree.

These things might soon be theirs no longer. Those shafts and pools of light, the tree, the graceful iron, might soon be viewed possessively by different eyes.

Papa was to have gone that noon, during his lunch hour, to the office of the Home Owners' Loan. If he had not succeeded in getting another extension, they would be leaving this house in which they had lived for more than fourteen years. There was little hope. The Home Owners' Loan was hard. They sat, making their plans.

"We'll be moving into a nice flat somewhere," said Mama. "Somewhere on South Park, or Michigan, or in Washington Park Court." Those flats, as the girls and Mama knew well, were burdens on wages twice the size of Papa's. This was not mentioned now.

"They're much prettier than this old house," said Helen. "I have friends I'd just as soon not bring here. And I have other friends that wouldn't come down this far for anything, unless they were in a taxi."

Yesterday, Maud Martha would have attacked

her. Tomorrow she might. Today she said nothing. She merely gazed at a little hopping robin in the tree, her tree, and tried to keep the fronts of her eyes dry.

"Well, I do know," said Mama, turning her hands over and over, "that I've been getting tireder and tireder of doing that firing. From October to April, there's firing to be done."

"But lately we've been helping, Harry and I," said Maud Martha. "And sometimes in March and April and in October, and even in November, we could build a little fire in the fireplace. Sometimes the weather was just right for that."

She knew, from the way they looked at her, that this had been a mistake. They did not want to cry.

But she felt that the little line of white, somewhat ridged with smoked purple, and all that cream-shot saffron, would never drift across any western sky except that in back of this house. The rain would drum with as sweet a dullness nowhere but here. The birds on South Park were mechanical birds, no better than the poor caught canaries in those "rich" women's sun parlors.

"It's just going to kill Papa!" burst out Maud Martha. "He loves this house! He *lives* for this house!"

"He lives for us," said Helen. "It's us he loves. He wouldn't want the house, except for us."

"And he'll have us," added Mama, "wherever."

"You know," Helen sighed, "if you want to know the truth, this is a relief. If this hadn't come up, we would have gone on, just dragged on, hanging out here forever."

"It might," allowed Mama, "be an act of God. God may just have reached down, and picked up the reins."

"Yes," Maud Martha cracked in, "that's what you always say—that God knows best."

Her mother looked at her quickly, decided the statement was not suspect, looked away.

Helen saw Papa coming. "There's Papa," said Helen.

They could not tell a thing from the way Papa

was walking. It was that same dear little staccato walk, one shoulder down, then the other, then repeat, and repeat. They watched his progress. He passed the Kennedys', he passed the vacant lot, he passed Mrs. Blakemore's. They wanted to hurl themselves over the fence, into the street, and shake the truth out of his collar. He opened his gate—the gate—and still his stride and face told them nothing.

"Hello," he said.

Mama got up and followed him through the front door. The girls knew better than to go in too.

Presently Mama's head emerged. Her eyes were lamps turned on.

"It's all right," she exclaimed. "He got it. It's all over. Everything is all right."

The door slammed shut. Mama's footsteps hurried away.

"I think," said Helen, rocking rapidly, "I think I'll give a party. I haven't given a party since I was eleven. I'd like some of my friends to just casually see that we're homeowners."

9

Helen

WHAT she remembered was Emmanuel; laughing, glinting in the sun; kneeing his wagon toward them, as they walked tardily home from school. Six years ago.

"How about a ride?" Emmanuel had hailed.

She had, daringly—it was not her way, not her native way—made a quip. A "sophisticated" quip. "Hi, handsome!" Instantly he had scowled, his dark face darkening.

"I don't mean you, you old black gal," little Emmanuel had exclaimed. "I mean Helen."

He had meant Helen, and Helen on the reissue of the invitation had climbed, without a word, into the wagon and was off and away.

Even now, at seventeen—high school graduate, mistress of her fate, and a ten-dollar-a-week file clerk in the very Forty-seventh Street lawyer's office where Helen was a fifteen-dollar-a-week typist—as she sat on Helen's bed and watched Helen primp for a party, the memory hurt. There was no consolation in the thought that not now and not then would she have *had* Emmanuel "off a Christmas tree." For the basic situation had never changed. Helen was still the one they wanted in the wagon, still "the pretty one," "the dainty one." The lovely one.

She did not know what it was. She had tried to find the something that must be there to imitate, that she might imitate it. But she did not know what it was. I wash as much as Helen does, she thought. My hair is longer and thicker, she thought. I'm much smarter. I read books and newspapers and old folks like to talk with me, she thought.

But the kernel of the matter was that, in spite of these things, she was poor, and Helen was still the ranking queen, not only with the Emmanuels of the world, but even with their father—their mother—their brother. She did not blame the family. It was not their fault. She understood. They could not help it. They were enslaved, were fascinated, and they were not at all to blame.

Her noble understanding of their blamelessness did not make any easier to bear such a circumstance as Harry's springing to open a door so that Helen's soft little hands might not have to cope with the sullyings of a doorknob, or running her errands, to save the sweet and fine little feet, or shouldering Helen's part against Maud Martha. Especially could these items burn when Maud Martha recalled her comradely rompings with Harry, watched by the gentle Helen from the clean and gentle harbor of the porch: take the day, for example, when Harry had been chased by those five big boys from Forty-first and Wabash, cursing, smelling, beastlike boys! with bats and rocks, and little stones that were more worrying than rocks; on that occasion out Maud Martha had dashed, when she saw from the front-room window Harry, panting and torn, racing for home; out she had dashed and down into the street with one of the smaller porch chairs held high over her head, and while Harry gained first the porch and next the safety side of the front door she had swung left, swung right, clouting a head here, a head there, and screaming at the top of her lungs, "Y' leave my brother alone! Y' leave my brother alone!" And who had washed those bloody wounds, and afterward vaselined them down? Really—in spite of everything she could not understand why Harry had to hold open doors for Helen, and calmly let them slam in her, Maud Martha's, his friend's, face.

It did not please her either, at the breakfast table, to watch her father drink his coffee and contentedly think (oh, she knew it!), as Helen started on her grapefruit, how daintily she ate, how gracefully she sat in her chair, how pure was her robe and unwrinkled, how neatly she had arranged her hair. Their father preferred Helen's hair to Maud Martha's (Maud Martha knew), which impressed him, not with its length and body, but simply with its apparent untamableness; for he would never get over that zeal of his for order in all things, in character, in housekeeping, in his own labor, in grooming, in human relationships. Always he had worried about Helen's homework, Helen's health. And now that boys were taking her out, he believed not one of them worthy of her, not one of them good enough to receive a note of her sweet voice: he insisted that she be returned before midnight. Yet who was it who sympathized with him in his decision to remain, for the rest of his days, the simple janitor! when everyone else was urging him to get out, get prestige, make more money? Who was it who sympathized with him in his almost desperate love for this old house? Who followed him about, emotionally speaking, loving this, doting on that? The kitchen, for instance, that was not beautiful in any way! The walls and ceilings, that were cracked. The chairs, which cried when people sat in them. The tables, that grieved audibly if anyone rested more than two fingers upon them. The huge cabinets, old and tired (when you shut their doors or drawers there was a sick, bickering little sound). The radiators, high and hideous. And underneath the low sink-coiled unlovely pipes, that Helen said made her think of a careless woman's underwear, peeping out. In fact, often had Helen given her opinion, unasked, of the whole house, of the whole "hulk of rotten wood." Often had her cool and gentle eyes sneered, gently and coolly, at her father's determination to hold his poor estate. But take that kitchen, for instance! Maud Martha, taking it, saw herself there, up and down her seventeen years, eating apples after school; making sweet potato tarts; drawing, on the pathetic table, the horse that won her the sixth grade prize; getting her hair curled for her first party, at that stove; washing dishes by summer twilight, with the back door wide open; making cheese and peanut butter sandwiches for a picnic. And even crying, crying in that pantry, when no one knew. The old sorrows brought there!—now dried, flattened out, breaking into interesting dust at the merest look. . . .

"You'll never get a boy friend," said Helen, fluffing on her Golden Peacock powder, "if you don't stop reading those books."

10

first beau

HE had a way of putting his hands on a Woman. Light, but perforating. Passing by, he would touch the Woman's hair, he would give the Woman's hair a careless, and yet deliberate, caress, working down from the top to the ends, then gliding to the chin, then lifting the chin till the poor female's eyes were forced to meet his, then proceeding down the neck. Maud Martha had watched this technique time after time, privately swearing that if he ever tried it on her she would settle him soon enough. Finally he had tried it, and a sloppy feeling had filled her, and she had not settled him at all. Not that she was thereafter, like the others, his to command, flatter, neglect, swing high, swing low, smooth with a grin, wrinkle with a scowl, just as his fancy wished. For Russell lacked—what? He was—nice. He was fun to go about with. He was decorated inside and out. He did things, said things, with a flourish. That was what he was. He was a flourish. He was a dazzling, long, and sleepily swishing flourish. "He will never be great," Maud Martha thought. "But he wouldn't be hurt if anybody told him that—if possible to choose from two, he would without hesitation choose being grand."

There he sat before her, in a sleeveless yellow-tan sweater and white, open-collared sport shirt, one leg thrust sexily out, fist on that hip, brown eyes ablaze, chin thrust up at her entrance as if *it* were to give her greeting, devil-like smile making her blink.

11

second beau

AND—don't laugh—he wanted a dog.

A picture of the English country gentleman. Roaming the rustic hill. He had not yet bought a pipe. He would immediately.

There already was the herringbone tweed. (Although old sensuousness, old emotional daring broke out at the top of the trousers, where there was that gathering, that kicked-back yearning toward the pleat!) There was the tie a man might think about for an hour before entering that better shop, in order to be able to deliberate only a sharp two minutes at the counter, under the icy estimate of the salesman. Here were the socks, here was the haircut, here were the shoes. The educated smile, the slight bow, the faint imperious nod. He belonged to the world of the university.

He was taking a number of loose courses on the Midway.

His scent was withdrawn, expensive, as he strode down the worn carpet of her living room, as though it were the educated green of the Midway.

He considered Parrington's *Main Currents in American Thought*. He had not mastered it. Only recently, he announced, had he learned of its existence. "Three volumes of the most reasonable approaches!—Yet there are chaps on that campus—*young!*—younger than I am—who read it years ago, who know it, who have had it for themselves for years, who have been seeing it on their fathers' shelves since infancy. They heard it discussed at the dinner table when they were four. As a ball is to me, so Parrington is to them. They've been kicking him around for years, like a *foot*ball!"

The idea agitated. His mother had taken in washing. She had had three boys, whom she sent to school clean but patched-up. Just so they were clean, she had said. That was all that mattered, she had said. She had said "ain't." She had said, "I ain't stud'n you." His father—he hadn't said anything at all.

He himself had had a paper route. Had washed windows, cleaned basements, sanded furniture, shoveled snow, hauled out trash and garbage for the neighbors. He had worked before that, running errands for people when he was six. What chance did he have, he mused, what chance was there for anybody coming out of a set of conditions that never allowed for the prevalence of sensitive, and intellectual, yet almost frivolous, dinner-table discussions of Parrington across four-year-old heads?

Whenever he left the Midway, said David McKemster, he was instantly depressed. East of Cottage Grove, people were clean, going somewhere that mattered, not talking unless they had something to say. West of the Midway, they leaned against buildings and their mouths were opening and closing very fast but nothing important was coming out. What did they know about Aristotle? The unhappiness he felt over there was physical. He wanted to throw up. There was a fence on Forty-seventh and—Champlain? Langley? Forestville?—he forgot what; broken, rotten, trying to lie down; and passing it on a windy night or on a night when it was drizzling, he felt lost, lapsed, negative, untended, extinguished, broken and lying down too—unappeasable. And looking up in those kitchenette windows, where the lights were dirty through dirty glass—they *could* wash the windows —was not at all "interesting" to him as it probably was to those guys at the university who had—who had—

Made a football out of Parrington.

Because he knew what it was. He knew it was a mess! He knew it wasn't "colorful," "exotic," "fascinating."

He wanted a dog. A good dog. No mongrel. An apartment—well-furnished, containing a good bookcase, filled with good books in good bindings. He wanted a phonograph, and records. The symphonies. And Yehudi Menuhin. He wanted some good art. These things were not extras. They went to make up a good background. The kind of background those guys had.

12

Maud Martha and New York

THE name "New York" glittered in front of her like the silver in the shops on Michigan Boulevard. It was silver, and it was solid, and it was remote: it was behind glass, it was behind bright glass like the silver in the shops. It was not for her. Yet.

When she was out walking, and with grating iron swish a train whipped by, off, above, its passengers were always, for her comfort, New York-bound. She sat inside with them. She leaned back in the plush. She sped, past farms, through tiny towns, where people slept, kissed, quarreled, ate midnight snacks; unfortunate folk who were not New York-bound and never would be.

Maud Martha loved it when her magazines said "New York," described "good" objects there, wonderful people there, recalled fine talk, the bristling or the creamy or the tactfully shimmering ways of life. They showed pictures of rooms with wood paneling, softly glowing, touched up by the compliment of a spot of auburn here, the low burn of a rare binding there. There were ferns in these rooms, and Chinese boxes; bits of dreamlike crystal; a taste of leather. In the advertisement pages, you saw where you could buy six Italian plates for eleven hundred dollars—and you must hurry, for there was just the one set; you saw where you could buy antique French bisque figurines (pale blue and gold) for—for— Her whole body become a hunger, she would pore over these pages. The clothes interested her, too; especially did she care for the pictures of women wearing carelessly, as if they were rags, dresses that were plain but whose prices were not. And the foolish food (her mother's description) enjoyed by New Yorkers fascinated her. They paid ten dollars for an eight-ounce jar of Russian caviar; they ate things called anchovies, and capers; they ate little diamond-shaped cheeses that paprika had but breathed on; they ate bitter-almond macaroons; they ate papaya packed in rum and syrup; they ate peculiar sauces, were free with honey, were lavish with butter, wine and cream.

She bought the New York papers downtown, read of the concerts and plays, studied the book reviews, was intent over the announcements of auctions. She liked the sound of "Fifth Avenue," "Town Hall," "B. Altman," "Hammacher Schlemmer." She was on Fifth Avenue whenever she wanted to be, and she it was who rolled up, silky or furry, in the taxi, was assisted out, and stood, her next step nebulous, before the theaters of the thousand lights, before velvet-lined impossible shops; she it was.

New York, for Maud Martha, was a symbol. Her

idea of it stood for what she felt life ought to be. Jeweled. Polished. Smiling. Poised. Calmly rushing! Straight up and down, yet graceful enough.

She thought of them drinking their coffee there —or tea, as in England. It was afternoon. Lustrous people glided over perfect floors, correctly smiling. They stopped before a drum table, covered with heavy white—and bearing a silver coffee service, old (in the better sense) china, a platter of orange and cinnamon cakes (or was it nutmeg the cakes would have in them?), sugar and cream, a Chinese box, one tall and slender flower. Their host or hostess poured, smiling too, nodding quickly to this one and that one, inquiring gently whether it should be sugar, or cream, or both, or neither. (She was teaching herself to drink coffee with neither.) All was *very* gentle. The voices, no matter how they rose, or even sharpened, had fur at the base. The steps never bragged, or grated in any way on any ear—not that they could very well, on so good a Persian rug, or deep soft carpeting. And the drum table stood in front of a screen, a Japanese one, perhaps, with rich and mellow, bread-textured colors. The people drank and nibbled, while they discussed the issues of the day, sorting, rejecting, revising. Then they went home, quietly, elegantly. They retired to homes not one whit less solid or embroidered than the home of their host or hostess.

What she wanted to dream, and dreamed, was her affair. It pleased her to dwell upon color and soft bready textures and light, on a complex beauty, on gemlike surfaces. What was the matter with that? Besides, who could safely swear that she would never be able to make her dream come true for herself? Not altogether, then!—but slightly?—in some part?

She was eighteen years old, and the world waited. To caress her.

13

low yellow

I KNOW what he is thinking, thought Maud Martha, as she sat on the porch in the porch swing with Paul Phillips. He is thinking that I am all right. That I am really all right. That I will do.

And I am glad of that, because my whole body is singing beside him. And when you feel like that beside a man you ought to be married to him.

I am what he would call—sweet.

But I am certainly not what he would call pretty. Even with all this hair (which I have just assured him, in response to his question, is not "natural," is not good grade or anything like good grade) even with whatever I have that puts a dimple in his heart, even with these nice ears, I am still, definitely, not what he can call pretty if he remains true to what his idea of pretty has always been. Pretty would be a little cream-colored thing with curly hair. Or at the very lowest pretty would be a little curly-haired thing the color of cocoa with a lot of milk in it. Whereas, I am the color of cocoa straight, if you can be even that "kind" to me.

He wonders, as we walk in the street, about the thoughts of the people who look at us. Are they thinking that he could do no better than—me? Then he thinks, Well, hmp! Well, huh!—all the little good-lookin' dolls that have wanted *him*—all the little sweet high-yellows that have ambled slowly past *his* front door—What he would like to tell those secretly snickering ones!—That any day out of the week he can do better than this black gal.

And by my own admission my hair is absolutely knappy.

"Fatherhood," said Paul, "is not exactly in my line. But it would be all right to have a couple or so of kids, good-looking, in my pocket, so to speak."

"I am not a pretty woman," said Maud Martha. "If you married a pretty woman, you could be the father of pretty children. Envied by people. The father of beautiful children."

"But I don't know," said Paul. "Because my features aren't fine. They aren't regular. They're heavy. They're real Negro features. I'm light, or at least I can claim to be a sort of low-toned yellow, and my hair has a teeny crimp. But even so I'm not handsome."

No, there would be little "beauty" getting born out of such a union.

Still, mused Maud Martha, I am what he would call—sweet, and I am good, and he will marry me. Although, he will be thinking, that's what he always says about letting yourself get interested in these incorruptible virgins, that so often your manhood will not let you concede defeat, and before you know it, you have let them steal you, put an end, perhaps, to your career.

He will fight, of course. He will decide that he must think a long time before he lets that happen here.

But in the end I'll hook him, even while he's wondering how this marriage will cramp him or pinch at him—at him, admirer of the gay life, spiffy clothes, beautiful yellow girls, natural hair, smooth cars, jewels, night clubs, cocktail lounges, class.

14

everybody will be surprised

"OF course," said Paul, "we'll have to start small. But it won't be very long before everybody will be surprised."

Maud Martha smiled.

"Your apartment, eventually, will be a dream. The *Defender* will come and photograph it." Paul grinned when he said that, but quite literally he believed it. Since he had decided to go ahead and marry her, he meant to "do it up right." People were going to look at his marriage and see only things to want. He was going to have a swanky flat. He and Maudie were going to dress well. They would entertain a lot.

"Listen," said Paul eagerly, "at a store on Forty-third and Cottage they're selling four rooms of furniture for eighty-nine dollars."

Maud Martha's heart sank.

"We'll go look at it tomorrow," added Paul.

"Paul—do you think we'll have a hard time finding a nice place—when the time comes?"

"No. I don't think so. But look here. I think we ought to plan on a stove-heated flat. We could get one of those cheap."

"Oh, I wouldn't like that. I've always lived in steam."

"I've always lived in stove—till a year ago. It's just as warm. And about fifteen dollars cheaper."

"Then what made your folks move to steam, then?"

"Ma wanted to live on a better-looking street. But we can't think about foolishness like that, when we're just starting out. Our flat will be hot stuff; the important thing is the flat, not the street; we can't study about foolishness like that; but our flat will be hot stuff. We'll have a swell flat."

"When you have stove heat, you have to have those ugly old fat black pipes stretching out all over the room."

"You don't just have to have long ones."

"I don't want any ones."

"You can have a little short one. And the new heaters they got look like radios. You'll like 'em."

Maud Martha silently decided she wouldn't, and resolved to hold out firmly against stove-heated flats. No stove-heated flats. And no basements. You got T.B. in basements.

"If you think a basement would be better—" began Paul.

"I don't," she interrupted.

"Basements are cheap too."

Was her attitude unco-operative? Should she be wanting to sacrifice more, for the sake of her man? A procession of pioneer women strode down her imagination; strong women, bold; praiseworthy, faithful, stout-minded; with a stout light beating in the eyes. Women who could stand low temperatures. Women who would toil eminently, to improve the lot of their men. Women who cooked. She thought of herself, dying for her man. It was a beautiful thought.

15

the kitchenette

THEIR home was on the third floor of a great gray stone building. The two rooms were small. The bedroom was furnished with a bed and dresser, old-fashioned, but in fair condition, and a faded occasional chair. In the kitchen were an oilcloth-covered table, two kitchen chairs, one folding chair, a cabinet base, a brown wooden icebox, and a three-burner gas stove. Only one of the burners worked, the housekeeper told them. The janitor would fix the others before they moved in. Maud Martha said she could fix them herself.

"Nope," objected Paul. "The janitor'll do it. That's what they pay him for." There was a bathroom at the end of the hall, which they would have to share with four other families who lived on the floor.

The housekeeper at the kitchenette place did not require a reference. . . .

The *Defender* would never come here with cameras.

Still, Maud Martha was, at first, enthusiastic. She made plans for this home. She would have the janitor move the bed and dresser out, tell Paul to buy a studio couch, a desk chest, a screen, a novelty chair, a white Venetian blind for the first room, and a green one for the kitchen, since the wallpaper there was green (with little red fishes swimming about). Perhaps they could even get a rug. A green one. And green drapes for the windows. Why, this *might* even turn out to be their dream apartment. It was small, but wonders could be wrought here. They could open up an account at L. Fish Furniture Store, pay a little every month. In that way, they could have the essentials right away. Later, they could get a Frigidaire. A baby's bed, when one became necessary, could go behind the screen, and they would have a pure living room.

Paul, after two or three weeks, told her sheepishly that kitchenettes were not so bad. Theirs seemed "cute and cozy" enough, he declared, and for his part, he went on, he was ready to "camp right down" until the time came to "build." Sadly, however, by that time Maud Martha had lost interest in the place, because the janitor had said that the Owner would not allow the furniture to be disturbed. Tenants moved too often. It was not worth the Owner's financial while to make changes, or to allow tenants to make them. They would have to be satisfied with "the apartment" as it was.

Then, one month after their installation, the first roach arrived. Ugly, shiny, slimy, slick-moving.

the kitchenette

She had rather see a rat—well, she had rather see a mouse. She had never yet been able to kill a roach. She could not bear to touch one, with foot or stick or twisted paper. She could only stand helpless, frozen, and watch the slick movement suddenly appear and slither, looking doubly evil, across the mirror, before which she had been calmly brushing her hair. And why? Why was he here? For she was scrubbing with water containing melted American Family soap and Lysol every other day.

And these things—roaches, and having to be satisfied with the place as it was—were not the only annoyances that had to be reckoned with. She was becoming aware of an oddness in color and sound and smell about her, the color and sound and smell of the kitchenette building. The color was gray, and the smell and sound had taken on a suggestion of the properties of color, and impressed one as gray, too. The sobbings, the frustrations, the small hates, the large and ugly hates, the little pushing-through love, the boredom, that came to her from behind those walls (some of them beaver-board) via speech and scream and sigh—all these were gray. And the smells of various types of sweat, and of bathing and bodily functions (the bathroom was always in use, someone was always in the bathroom) and of fresh or stale love-making, which rushed in thick fumes to your nostrils as you walked down the hall, or down the stairs—these were *gray.*

There was a whole lot of grayness here.

16

the young couple at home

PAUL had slept through most of the musicale. Three quarters of the time his head had been a heavy knot on her shoulder. At each of her attempts to remove it, he had waked up so suddenly, and had given her a look of such childlike fierceness, that she could only smile.

Now on the streetcar, however—the car was in the garage—he was not sleepy, and he kept "amusing" Maud Martha with little "tricks," such as cocking his head archly and winking at her, or digging her slyly in the ribs, or lifting her hand to his lips, and blowing on it softly, or poking a finger under her chin and raising it awkwardly, or feeling her muscle, then putting her hand on his muscle, so that she could tell the difference. Such as that. "Clowning," he called it. And because he felt that he was making her happy, she tried not to see the uncareful stares and smirks of the other passengers—uncareful and insultingly consolatory. He sat playfully upon part of her thigh. He gently kicked her toe.

Once home, he went immediately to the bathroom. He did not try to mask his need, he was obvious and direct about it.

"He could make," she thought, "a comment or two on what went on at the musicale. Or some little joke. It isn't that I'm unreasonable or stupid. But everything can be done with a little grace. I'm sure of it."

When he came back, he yawned, stretched, smeared his lips up and down her neck, assured her of his devotion, and sat down on the bed to take off his shoes. She picked up *Of Human Bondage,* and sat at the other end of the bed.

"Snuggle up," he invited.

"I thought I'd read awhile."

"I guess I'll read awhile, too," he decided, when his shoes were off and had been kicked into the kitchen. She got up, went to the shoes, put them in the closet. He grinned at her merrily. She was conscious of the grin, but refused to look at him. She went back to her book. He settled down to his. His was a paper-backed copy of *Sex in the Married Life.*

There he sat, slouched down, terribly absorbed, happy in his sock feet, curling his toes inside the socks.

"I want you to read this book," he said, "—but at the right times: one chapter each night before retiring." He reached over, pinched her on the buttock.

She stood again. "Shall I make some cocoa?" she asked pleasantly. "And toast some sandwiches?"

"Say, I'd like that," he said, glancing up briefly.

She toasted rye strips spread with pimento cheese and grated onion. She made cocoa.

They ate, drank, and read together. She read *Of Human Bondage.* He read *Sex in the Married Life.* They were silent.

Five minutes passed. She looked at him. He was asleep. His head had fallen back, his mouth was open—it was a good thing there were no flies—his ankles were crossed. And the feet!—pointing confidently out (no one would harm them). *Sex in the Married Life* was about to slip to the floor. She did not stretch out a hand to save it.

Once she had taken him to a library. While occupied with the card cases she had glanced up, had observed that he, too, was busy among the cards. "Do you want a book?" "No-o. I'm just curious about something. I wondered if there could be a man in the world named Bastard. Sure enough, there is."

Paul's book fell, making a little clatter. But he did not wake up, and she did not get up.

17

Maud Martha spares the mouse

THERE. She had it at last. The weeks it had devoted to eluding her, the tricks, the clever hide-and-go-seeks, the routes it had in all sobriety devised, together with the delicious moments it had, undoubtedly, laughed up its sleeve—all to no ultimate avail. She had that mouse.

It shook its little self, as best it could, in the trap. Its bright black eyes contained no appeal—the little creature seemed to understand that there was no hope of mercy from the eternal enemy, no hope of reprieve or postponement—but a fine small dignity. It waited. It looked at Maud Martha.

She wondered what else it was thinking. Perhaps that there was not enough food in its larder. Perhaps that little Betty, a puny child from the start, would not, now, be getting fed. Perhaps that, now, the family's seasonal house-cleaning, for lack of expert direction, would be left undone. It might be regretting that young Bobby's education was now at an end. It might be nursing personal regrets. No more the mysterious shadows of the kitchenette, the uncharted twists, the unguessed halls. No more the sweet delights of the chase, the charms of being unsuccessfully hounded, thrown at.

Maud Martha could not bear the little look.

"Go home to your children," she urged. "To your wife or husband." She opened the trap. The mouse vanished.

Suddenly, she was conscious of a new cleanness in her. A wide air walked in her. A life had blundered its way into her power and it had been hers to preserve or destroy. She had not destroyed. In the center of that simple restraint was—creation. She had created a piece of life. It was wonderful.

"Why," she thought, as her height doubled, "why, I'm good! I am *good.*"

She ironed her aprons. Her back was straight. Her eyes were mild, and soft with a godlike loving-kindness.

18

we're the only colored people here

WHEN they went out to the car there were just the very finest bits of white powder coming down with an almost comical little ethereal hauteur, to add themselves to the really important, piled-up masses of their kind.

And it wasn't cold.

Maud Martha laughed happily to herself. It was pleasant out, and tonight she and Paul were very close to each other.

He held the door open for her—instead of going

on around to the driving side, getting in, and leaving her to get in at her side as best she might. When he took this way of calling her "lady" and informing her of his love she felt precious, protected, delicious. She gave him an excited look of gratitude. He smiled indulgently.

"Want it to be the Owl again?"

"Oh, no no, Paul. Let's not go there tonight. I feel too good inside for that. Let's go downtown?"

She had to suggest that with a question mark at the end, always. He usually had three protests. Too hard to park. Too much money. Too many white folks. And tonight she could almost certainly expect a no, she feared, because he had come out in his blue work shirt. There was a spot of apricot juice on the collar, too. His shoes were not shined. . . . But he nodded!

"We've never been to the World Playhouse," she said cautiously. "They have a good picture. I'd feel rich in there."

"You really wanta?"

"Please?"

"Sure."

It wasn't like other movie houses. People from the Studebaker Theatre which, as Maud Martha whispered to Paul, was "all-locked-arms" with the World Playhouse, were strolling up and down the lobby, laughing softly, smoking with gentle grace.

"There must be a play going on in there and this is probably an intermission," Maud Martha whispered again.

"I don't know why you feel you got to whisper," whispered Paul. "Nobody else is whispering in here." He looked around, resentfully, wanting to see a few, just a few, colored faces. There were only their own.

Maud Martha laughed a nervous defiant little laugh; and spoke loudly. "There certainly isn't any reason to whisper. Silly, huh."

The strolling women were cleverly gowned. Some of them had flowers or flashers in their hair. They looked—cooked. Well cared-for. And as though they had never seen a roach or a rat in their lives. Or gone without heat for a week. And the men had even edges. They were men, Maud Martha thought, who wouldn't stoop to fret over less than a thousand dollars.

"We're the only colored people here," said Paul.

She hated him a little. "Oh, hell. Who in hell cares."

"Well, what I want to know is, where do you pay the damn fares."

"There's the box office. Go on up."

He went on up. It was closed.

"Well," sighed Maud Martha, "I guess the picture has started already. But we can't have missed much. Go on up to that girl at the candy counter and ask her where we should pay our money."

He didn't want to do that. The girl was lovely and blonde and cold-eyed, and her arms were akimbo, and the set of her head was eloquent. No one else was at the counter.

"Well. We'll wait a minute. And see—"

Maud Martha hated him again. Coward. She ought to flounce over to the girl herself—show him up. . . .

The people in the lobby tried to avoid looking curiously at two shy Negroes wanting desperately not to seem shy. The white women looked at the Negro woman in her outfit with which no special fault could be found, but which made them think, somehow, of close rooms, and wee, close lives. They looked at her hair. They liked to see a dark colored girl with long, long hair. They were always slightly surprised, but agreeably so, when they did. They supposed it was the hair that had got her that yellowish, good-looking Negro man.

The white men tried not to look at the Negro man in the blue work shirt, the Negro man without a tie.

An usher opened a door of the World Playhouse part and ran quickly down the few steps that led from it to the lobby. Paul opened his mouth.

"Say, fella. Where do we get the tickets for the movie?"

The usher glanced at Paul's feet before answering. Then he said coolly, but not unpleasantly, "I'll take the money."

we're the only colored people here

They were able to go in.

And the picture! Maud Martha was so glad that they had not gone to the Owl! Here was technicolor, and the love story was sweet. And there was classical music that silvered its way into you and made your back cold. And the theater itself! It was no palace, no such Great Shakes as the Tivoli out south, for instance (where many colored people went every night). But you felt good sitting there, yes, good, and as if, when you left it, you would be going home to a sweet-smelling apartment with flowers on little gleaming tables; and wonderful silver on night-blue velvet, in chests; and crackly sheets; and lace spreads on such beds as you saw at Marshall Field's. Instead of back to your kit'n't apt., with the garbage of your floor's families in a big can just outside your door, and the gray sound of little gray feet scratching away from it as you drag up those flights of narrow complaining stairs.

Paul pressed her hand. Paul said, "We oughta do this more often."

And again. "We'll have to do this more often. And go to plays, too. I mean at that Blackstone, and Studebaker."

She pressed back, smiling beautifully to herself in the darkness. Though she knew that once the spell was over it would be a year, two years, more, before he would return to the World Playhouse. And he might never go to a real play. But she was learning to love moments. To love moments for themselves.

When the picture was over, and the lights revealed them for what they were, the Negroes stood up among the furs and good cloth and faint perfume, looked about them eagerly. They hoped they would meet no cruel eyes. They hoped no one would look intruded upon. They had enjoyed the picture so, they were so happy, they wanted to laugh, to say warmly to the other outgoers, "Good, huh? Wasn't it swell?"

This, of course, they could not do. But if only no one would look intruded upon. . . .

19

if you're light and have long hair

CAME the invitation that Paul recognized as an honor of the first water, and as sufficient indication that he was, at last, a social somebody. The invitation was from the Foxy Cats Club, the club of clubs. He was to be present, in formal dress, at the Annual Foxy Cats Dawn Ball. No chances were taken: "Top hat, white tie and tails" hastily followed the "Formal dress," and that elucidation was in bold type.

Twenty men were in the Foxy Cats Club. All were good-looking. All wore clothes that were rich and suave. All "handled money," for their number consisted of well-located barbers, policemen, "government men" and men with a lucky touch at the tracks. Certainly the Foxy Cats Club was not a representative of that growing group of South Side organizations devoted to moral and civic improvements, or to literary or other cultural pursuits. If that had been so, Paul would have chucked his bid (which was black and silver, decorated with winking cat faces) down the toilet with a yawn. "That kind of stuff" was hardly understood by Paul, and was always dismissed with an airy "dicty," "hincty" or "high-falutin'." But no. The Foxy Cats devoted themselves solely to the business of being "hep," and each year they spent hundreds of dollars on their wonderful Dawn Ball, which did not begin at dawn, but was scheduled to end at dawn. "Ball," they called the frolic, but it served also the purposes of party, feast and fashion show. Maud Martha, watching him study his invitation, watching him lift his chin, could see that he considered himself one of the blessed.

Who—what kind soul had recommended him!

"He'll have to take me," thought Maud Martha. "For the envelope is addressed 'Mr. and Mrs.,' and I opened it. I guess he'd like to leave me home. At the Ball, there will be only beautiful girls, or real stylish ones. There won't be more than a handful like me. My type is not a Foxy Cat favorite. But he can't avoid taking me—since he hasn't yet thought of words or ways strong enough, and at the same time soft enough—for he's kind: he doesn't like to injure—to carry across to me the news that he is not to be held permanently by my type, and that he can go on with this marriage only if I put no ropes or questions around him. Also, he'll want to humor me, now that I'm pregnant."

She would need a good dress. That, she knew, could be a problem, on his grocery clerk's pay. He would have his own expenses. He would have to rent his topper and tails, and he would have to buy a fine tie, and really excellent shoes. She knew he was thinking that on the strength of his appearance and sophisticated behavior at this Ball might depend his future admission (for why not dream?) to *membership,* actually, in the Foxy Cats Club!

"I'll settle," decided Maud Martha, "on a plain white princess-style thing and some blue and black satin ribbon. I'll go to my mother's. I'll work miracles at the sewing machine.

"On that night, I'll wave my hair. I'll smell faintly of lily of the valley."

The main room of the Club 99, where the Ball was held, was hung with green and yellow and red balloons, and the thick pillars, painted to give an effect of marble, and stretching from floor to ceiling, were draped with green and red and yellow crepe paper. Huge ferns, rubber plants and bowls of flowers were at every corner. The floor itself was a decoration, golden, glazed. There was no overhead light; only wall lamps, and the bulbs in these were romantically dim. At the back of the room, standing on a furry white rug, was the long banquet table, dressed in damask, accented by groups of thin silver candlesticks bearing white candles, and laden with lovely food: cold chicken, lobster, candied ham fruit combinations, potato salad in a great gold dish, corn sticks, a cheese fluff in spiked tomato cups, fruit cake, angel cake, sunshine cake. The drinks were at a smaller table nearby, behind which stood a genial mixologist, quick with maraschino cherries, and with lemon, ice and liquor. Wines were there, and whiskey, and rum, and egg-nog made with pure cream.

Paul and Maud Martha arrived rather late, on purpose. Rid of their wraps, they approached the glittering floor. Bunny Bates's orchestra was playing Ellington's "Solitude."

Paul, royal in rented finery, was flushed with excitement. Maud Martha looked at him. Not very tall. Not very handsomely made. But there was that extraordinary quality of maleness. Hiding in the body that was not *too* yellow, waiting to spring out at her, surround her (she liked to think) —that maleness. The Ball stirred her. The Beauties, in their gorgeous gowns, bustling, supercilious; the young men, who at other times most unpleasantly blew their noses, and darted surreptitiously into alleys to relieve themselves, and sweated and swore at their jobs, and scratched their more intimate parts, now smiling, smooth, overgallant; the drowsy lights; the smells of food and flowers, the smell of Murray's pomade, the body perfumes, natural and superimposed; the sensuous heaviness of the wine-colored draperies at the many windows; the music, now steamy and slow, now as clear and fragile as glass, now raging, passionate, now moaning and thickly gray. The Ball made toys of her emotions, stirred her variously. But she was anxious to have it end, she was anxious to be at home again, with the door closed behind herself and her husband. Then, he might be warm. There might be more than the absent courtesy he had been giving her of late. Then, he might be the tree she had a great need to lean against, in this "emergency." There was no telling what dear thing he might say to her, what little gem let fall.

But, to tell the truth, his behavior now was not very promising of gems to come. After their second dance he escorted her to a bench by the wall, left her. Trying to look nonchalant, she sat. She sat, trying not to show the inferiority she did not feel. When the music struck up again, he began to dance with someone red-haired and curved, and white as a white. Who was she? He had approached her easily, he had taken her confidently, he held her and conversed with her as though he had known her well for a long, long time. The girl smiled up at him. Her gold-spangled bosom was pressed—was pressed against that maleness—

A man asked Maud Martha to dance. He was dark, too. His mustache was small.

"Is this your first Foxy Cats?" he asked.

"What?" Paul's cheek was on that of Gold-Spangles.

"First Cats?"

"Oh. Yes." Paul and Gold-Spangles were weaving through the noisy twisting couples, were trying, apparently, to get to the reception hall.

"Do you know that girl? What's her name?" Maud Martha asked her partner, pointing to Gold-Spangles. Her partner looked, nodded. He pressed her closer.

"That's Maella. That's Maella."

"Pretty, isn't she?" She wanted him to keep talking about Maella. He nodded again.

"Yep. She has 'em howling along the stroll, all right, all right."

Another man, dancing past with an artificial redhead, threw a whispered word at Maud Martha's partner, who caught it eagerly, winked. "Solid, ol' man," he said. "Solid, Jack." He pressed Maud Martha closer. "You're a babe," he said. "You're a real babe." He reeked excitingly of tobacco, liquor, pinesoap, toilet water, and Sen Sen.

Maud Martha thought of her parents' back yard. Fresh. Clean. Smokeless. In her childhood, a snowball bush had shone there, big above the dandelions. The snowballs had been big, healthy. Once, she and her sister and brother had waited in the back yard for their parents to finish readying themselves for a trip to Milwaukee. The snowballs had been so beautiful, so fat and startlingly white in the sunlight, that she had suddenly loved home a thousand times more than ever before, and had not wanted to go to Milwaukee. But as the children grew, the bush sickened. Each year the snowballs were smaller and more dispirited. Finally a summer came when there were no blossoms at all. Maud Martha wondered what had become of the bush. For it was not there now. Yet she, at least, had never seen it go.

"Not," thought Maud Martha, "that they love each other. It oughta be that simple. Then I could lick it. It oughta be that easy. But it's my color that makes him mad. I try to shut my eyes to that, but it's no good. What I am inside, what is really me, he likes okay. But he keeps looking at my color, which is like a wall. He has to jump over it in order to meet and touch what I've got for him. He has to jump away up high in order to see it. He gets awful tired of all that jumping."

Paul came back from the reception hall. Maella was clinging to his arm. A final cry of the saxophone finished that particular slice of the blues. Maud Martha's partner bowed, escorted her to a chair by a rubber plant, bowed again, left.

"I could," considered Maud Martha, "go over there and scratch her upsweep down. I could spit on her back. I could scream. 'Listen,' I could scream, 'I'm making a baby for this man and I mean to do it in peace.' "

But if the root was sour what business did she have up there hacking at a leaf?

20

a birth

AFTER dinner, they washed dishes together. Then they undressed, and Paul got in bed, and was asleep almost instantly. She went down the long public hall to the bathroom, in her blue chenille robe. On her way back down the squeezing dark of the hall she felt—something softly separate in her. Back in the bedroom, she put on her gown, then stepped to the dresser to smear her face with cold cream. But when she turned around to get in the bed she couldn't move. Her legs cramped painfully, and she had a tremendous desire to eliminate which somehow she felt she would never be able to gratify.

"Paul!" she cried. As though in his dreams he had been waiting to hear that call, and that call only, he was up with a bound.

"I can't move."

He rubbed his eyes.

"Maudie, are you kidding?"

"I'm not kidding, Paul. I can't move."

He lifted her up and laid her on the bed, his eyes stricken.

"Look here, Maudie. Do you think you're going to have that baby tonight?"

"No—no. These are just what they call 'false pains.' I'm not going to have the baby tonight. Can you get—my gown off?"

"Sure. Sure."

But really he was afraid to touch her. She lay nude on the bed for a few moments, perfectly still. Then all of a sudden motion came to her. Whereas before she had not been able to move her legs, now she could not keep them still.

"Oh, my God," she prayed aloud. "Just let my legs get still five minutes." God did not answer the prayer.

Paul was pacing up and down the room in fright.

"Look here. I don't think those are false pains. I think you're going to have that baby tonight."

"Don't say that, Paul," she muttered between clenched teeth. "I'm not going to have the baby tonight."

"I'm going to call your mother."

"Don't do that, Paul. She can't stand to see things like this. Once she got a chance to see a still-born baby, but she fainted before they even unwrapped it. She can't stand to see things like this. False pains, that's all. Oh, God, why don't you let me keep my legs still!"

She began to whimper in a manner that made Paul want to vomit. His thoughts traveled to the girl he had met at the Dawn Ball several months before. Cool. Sweet. Well-groomed. Fair.

"You're going to have that baby *now*. I'm going down to call up your mother and a doctor."

"DON'T YOU GO OUT OF HERE AND LEAVE ME ALONE! Damn. DAMN!"

"All right. All right. I won't leave you alone. I'll get the woman next door to come in. But somebody's got to get a doctor here."

"Don't you sneak out! Don't you *sneak* out!" She was pushing down with her stomach now. Paul, standing at the foot of the bed with his hands in his pockets, saw the creeping insistence of what he thought was the head of the child.

"Oh, my Lord!" he cried. "It's coming! It's coming!"

He walked about the room several times. He went to the dresser and began to brush his hair. She looked at him in speechless contempt. He went out of the door, and ran down the three flights of stairs two or three steps at a time. The telephone was on the first floor. No sooner had he picked up the receiver than he heard Maud Martha give what he was sure could *only* be called a "bloodcurdling scream." He bolted up the stairs, saw her wriggling on the bed, said softly, "Be right back," and bolted down again. First he called his mother's doctor, and begged him to come right over. Then he called the Browns.

"Get her to the hospital!" shouted Belva Brown. "You'll have to get her to the hospital right away!"

"I can't. She's having the baby now. She isn't going to let anybody touch her. I tell you, she's having the baby."

"Don't be a fool. Of course she can get to the hospital. Why, she mustn't have it there in the house! I'm coming over there. I'll take her myself. Be sure there's plenty of gas in that car."

He tried to reach his mother. She was out—had not returned from a revival meeting.

When Paul ran back up the stairs, he found young Mrs. Cray, who lived in the front apartment of their floor, attending his shrieking wife.

"I heard 'er yellin', and thought I'd better come

in, seein' as how you all is so confused. Got a doctor comin'?"

Paul sighed heavily. "I just called one. Thanks for coming in. This—this came on all of a sudden, and I don't think I know what to do."

"Well, the thing to do is get a doctor right off. She's goin' to have the baby soon. Call *my* doctor." She gave him a number. "Whichever one gets here first can work on her. Ain't no time to waste."

Paul ran back down the stairs and called the number. "What's the doctor's address?" he yelled up. Mrs. Cray yelled it down. He went out to get the doctor personally. He was glad of an excuse to escape. He was sick of hearing Maudie scream. He had had no idea that she could scream that kind of screaming. It was awful. How lucky he was that he had been born a man. How lucky he was that he had been born a man!

Belva arrived in twenty minutes. She was grateful to find another woman present. She had come to force Maud Martha to start for the hospital, but a swift glance told her that the girl would not leave her bed for many days. As she said to her husband and Helen later on, "The baby was all ready to spill out."

When her mother came in the door Maud Martha tightened her lips, temporarily forgetful of her strange pain. (But it wasn't pain. It was something else.) "Listen. If you're going to make a fuss, go on out. I'm having enough trouble without you making a fuss over everything."

Mrs. Cray giggled encouragingly. Belva said bravely, "I'm not going to make a fuss. You'll see. Why, there's nothing to make a fuss *about*. You're just going to have a baby, like millions of other women. Why should I make a fuss?"

Maud Martha tried to smile but could not quite make it. The sensations were getting grindingly sharp. She screamed longer and louder, explaining breathlessly in between times, "I just can't help it. Excuse me."

"Why, go on and scream," urged Belva. "You're supposed to scream. That's your privilege. I'm sure *I* don't mind." Her ears were splitting, and over and over as she stood there looking down at her agonized daughter, she said to herself, "Why doesn't the doctor come? Why doesn't the doctor come? I know I'm going to faint." She and Mrs. Cray stood, one on each side of the bed, purposelessly holding a sheet over Maud Martha, under which they peeped as seldom as they felt was safe. Maud Martha kept asking, "Has the head come?" Presently she felt as though her whole body were having a bowel movement. The head came. Then, with a little difficulty, the wide shoulders. Then easily, with soft and slippery smoothness, out slipped the rest of the body and the baby was born. The first thing it did was sneeze.

Maud Martha laughed as though she could never bear to stop. "Listen to him sneeze. My little baby. Don't let him drown, Mrs. Cray." Mrs. Cray looked at Maud Martha, because she did not want to look at the baby. "How you know it's a him?" Maud Martha laughed again.

Belva also refused to look at the baby. "See, Maudie," she said, "see how brave I was? The baby is born, and I didn't get nervous or faint or anything. Didn't I tell you?"

"Now isn't that nice," thought Maud Martha. "Here I've had the baby, and she thinks I should praise her for having stood up there and looked on." Was it, she suddenly wondered, as hard to watch suffering as it was to bear it?

Five minutes after the birth, Paul got back with Mrs. Cray's doctor, a large silent man, who came in swiftly, threw the sheet aside without saying a word, cut the cord. Paul looked at the new human being. It appeared gray and greasy. Life was hard, he thought. What had he done to deserve a stillborn child? But there it was, lying dead.

"It's dead, isn't it?" he asked dully.

"Oh, get out of here!" cried Mrs. Cray, pushing him into the kitchen and shutting the door.

"Girl," said the doctor. Then grudgingly, "Fine girl."

"Did you hear what the doctor said, Maudie?" chattered Belva. "You've got a daughter, the doctor says." The doctor looked at her quickly.

"Say, you'd better go out and take a walk around the block. You don't look so well."

Gratefully, Belva obeyed. When she got back, Mrs. Cray and the doctor had oiled and dressed the baby—dressed her in an outfit found in Maud Martha's top dresser drawer. Belva looked at the newcomer in amazement.

"Well, she's a little beauty, isn't she!" she cried. She had not expected a handsome child.

Maud Martha's thoughts did not dwell long on the fact of the baby. There would be all her life long for that. She preferred to think, now, about how well she felt. Had she ever in her life felt so well? She felt well enough to get up. She folded her arms triumphantly across her chest, as another young woman, her neighbor to the rear, came in.

"Hello, Mrs. Barksdale!" she hailed. "Did you hear the news? I just had a baby, and I feel strong enough to go out and shovel coal! Having a baby is *nothing,* Mrs. Barksdale. Nothing at all."

"Aw, yeah?" Mrs. Barksdale smacked her gum admiringly. "Well, from what I heard back there a while ago, didn't seem like it was nothing. Girl, I didn't know anybody *could* scream that loud." Maud Martha tittered. Oh, she felt fine. She wondered why Mrs. Barksdale hadn't come in while the screaming was going on; she had missed it all.

People. Weren't they sweet. She had never said more than "Hello, Mrs. Barksdale" and "Hello, Mrs. Cray" to these women before. But as soon as something happened to her, in they trooped. People were sweet.

The doctor brought the baby and laid it in the bed beside Maud Martha. Shortly before she had heard it in the kitchen—a bright delight had flooded through her upon first hearing that part of Maud Martha Brown Phillips expressing itself with a voice of its own. But now the baby was quiet and returned its mother's stare with one that seemed equally curious and mystified but perfectly cool and undisturbed.

21

posts

PEOPLE have to choose something decently constant to depend on, thought Maud Martha. People must have something to lean on.

But the love of a single person was not enough. Not only was personal love itself, however good, a thing that varied from week to week, from second to second, but the parties to it were likely, for example, to die, any minute, or otherwise be parted, or destroyed. At any time.

Not alone was the romantic love of a man and a

woman fallible, but the breadier love between parents and children; brothers; animals; friend and friend. Those too could not be heavily depended on.

Could be nature, which had a seed, or root, or an element (what do you want to call it) of constancy, under all that system of change. Of course, to say "system" at all implied arrangement, and therefore some order of constancy.

Could be, she mused, a marriage. The marriage shell, not the romance, or love, it might contain. A marriage, the plainer, the more plateaulike, the better. A marriage made up of Sunday papers and shoeless feet, baking powder biscuits, baby baths, and matinees and laundrymen, and potato plants in the kitchen window.

Was, perhaps, the whole life of man a dedication to this search for something to lean upon, and was, to a great degree, his "happiness" or "unhappiness" written up for him by the demands or limitations of what he chose for that work?

For work it was. Leaning was a work.

22

tradition and Maud Martha

WHAT she had wanted was a solid. She had wanted shimmering form; warm, but hard as stone and as difficult to break. She had wanted to found—tradition. She had wanted to shape, for their use, for hers, for his, for little Paulette's, a set of falterless customs. She had wanted stone: here she was, being wife to *him*, salving him, in every way considering and replenishing him—in short, here she was celebrating Christmas night by passing pretzels and beer.

tradition and Maud Martha

He had done his part, was his claim. He had, had he not? lugged in a Christmas tree. So he had waited till early Christmas morning, when a tree was cheap; so he could not get the lights to burn; so the tinsel was insufficient and the gold balls few. He had promised a tree and he had gotten a tree, and that should be enough for everybody. Furthermore, Paulette had her blocks, her picture book, h[illegible] doll buggy and her doll. So the doll's left elbow was chipped: more than that would be chipped before Paulette was through! And if the doll buggy was not like the Gold Coast buggies, that was too bad; that was too, too bad for Maud Martha, for Paulette. Here he was, whipping himself to death daily, that Maud Martha's stomach and Paulette's stomach might receive bread and milk and navy beans with tomato catsup, and he was taken to task because he had not furnished, in addition, a velvet-lined buggy with white-walled wheels! Oh yes that *was* what Maud Martha wanted, for her precious princess daughter, and no use denying. But she could just get out and work, that was all. She could just get out and grab herself a job and buy some of these beans and buggies. And in the meantime, she could just help entertain his friends. She was his wife, and he was the head of the family, and on Christmas night the least he could do, by God, and *would* do, by God, was stand his friends a good mug of beer. And to heck with, in fact, to hell with, her fruitcakes and coffees. Put Paulette to bed.

At Home, the buying of the Christmas tree was a ritual. Always it had come into the Brown household four days before Christmas, tall, but not too tall, and not too wide. Tinsel, bulbs, little Santa Clauses and snowmen, and the pretty gold and silver and colored balls did not have to be renewed oftener than once in five years because after Christmas they were always put securely away, on a special shelf in the basement, where they rested for a year. Black walnut candy, in little flat white sheets, crunchy, accompanied the tree, but it was never eaten until Christmas eve. Then, late at night, a family decorating party was held, Maud

Martha, Helen and Harry giggling and teasing and occasionally handing up a ball or Santa Claus, while their father smiled benignly over all and strung and fitted and tinseled, and their mother brought in the black walnut candy and steaming cups of cocoa with whipped cream, and plain shortbread. And everything peaceful, sweet!

And there were the other customs. Easter customs. In childhood, never till Easter morning was "the change" made, the change from winter to spring underwear. Then, no matter how cold it happened to be, off came the heavy trappings and out, for Helen and Maud Martha, were set the new little patent leather shoes and white socks, the little b.v.d.'s and light petticoats, and for Harry, the new brown oxfords, and white shorts and sleeveless undershirts. The Easter eggs had always been dyed the night before, and in the morning, before Sunday school, the Easter baskets, full of chocolate eggs and candy bunnies and cotton bunnies, were handed round, but not eaten from until after Sunday school, and even then not much!—

because there was more candy coming, and dyed eggs, too, to be received (and eaten on the spot) at the Sunday School Children's Easter Program, on which every one of them recited until Maud Martha was twelve.

What of October customs?—of pumpkins yellowly burning; of polished apples in a water-green bowl; of sheets for ghost costumes, surrendered up by Mama with a sigh?

And birthdays, with their pink and white cakes and candles, strawberry ice cream, and presents wrapped up carefully and tied with wide ribbons: whereas here was this man, who never considered giving his own mother a birthday bouquet, and dropped in his wife's lap a birthday box of drugstore candy (when he thought of it) wrapped in the drugstore green.

The dinner table, at home, was spread with a white white cloth, cheap but white and very white, and whatever was their best in china sat in cheerful dignity, firmly arranged, upon it. This man was not a lover of tablecloths, he could eat from a splintery board, he could eat from the earth.

She passed round Blatz, and inhaled the smoke of the guests' cigarettes, and watched the soaked tissue that had enfolded the corner Chicken Inn's burned barbecue drift listlessly to her rug. She removed from her waist the arm of Chuno Jones, Paul's best friend.

23

kitchenette folks

OF the people in her building, Maud Martha was most amused by Oberto, who had the largest flat of all, a three-roomer on the first floor.

Oberto was a happy man. He had a nice little going grocery store. He had his health. And, most important, he had his little lovely wife Marie.

Some folks did not count Marie among his blessings. She never got up before ten. Oberto must prepare his breakfast or go breakfastless. As a rule, he made only coffee, leaving one cup of it in the pot for her. At ten or after, in beautiful solitude, she would rise, bathe and powder for an hour, then proceed to the kitchen, where she heated that coffee, fried bacon and eggs for herself, and toasted raisin bread.

Marie dusted and swept infrequently, scrubbed only when the floors were heavy with dirt and grease. Her meals were generally underdone or burned. She sent the laundry out every week, but more often than not left the clothes (damp) in the bag throughout the week, spilling them out a few minutes before she expected the laundryman's next call, that the bag might again be stuffed with dirty clothes and carried off. Oberto's shirts were finished at the laundry. Underwear he wore rough-dried. Her own clothes, however, she ironed with regularity and care.

Such domestic sins were shocking enough. But people accused her of yet more serious crimes. It was well thought on the south side that Oberto's wife was a woman of affairs, barely taking time to lay one down before she gathered up another. It was rumored, too, but not confirmed, that now and then she was obliged to make quiet calls of business on a certain Madame Lomiss, of Thirty-fourth and Calumet.

But Oberto was happy. The happiest man, he argued, in his community. True enough, Wilma, the wife of Magnicentius, the Thirty-ninth Street barber, baked rolls of white and fluffy softness. But Magnicentius himself could not deny that Wilma was a filthy woman, and wore stockings two days, at least, before she washed them. He even made no secret of the fact that she went to bed in ragged, dire, cotton nightgowns.

True, too, Viota, the wife of Leon, the Coca-Cola truck driver, not only ironed her husband's shirts, but did all the laundry work herself, beginning early every Monday morning—scrubbing the sheets, quilts, blankets, and slip covers with her own hefty hand. But Leon himself could not deny that Viota was a boisterous, big woman with a voice of wonderful power, and eyes of pink-streaked yellow and a nose that never left off sniffing.

Who, further, would question the truth that Nathalia, the wife of John the laundryman, kept her house shining, and smelling of Lysol and Gold Dust at all times, and that every single Saturday night she washed down the white walls of her perfect kitchen? But verily who (of an honorable tongue) could deny that the active-armed Nathalia had little or no acquaintance with the deodorant qualities of Mum, Hush, or Quiet?

Remembering Nathalia, and remembering Wilma and Viota, Oberto thanked his lucky stars that he had had sense enough to marry his dainty little Marie, who spoke in modulated tones (almost in a whisper), who wore filmy black nightgowns, who bathed always once and sometimes twice a day in water generously treated with sweet bath crystals, and fluffed herself all over with an expensive lavender talcum, and creamed her arms and legs with a rosy night cream, and powdered her face, that was reddish brown (like an Indian's!)

with a stuff that the movie stars preferred, and wore clothes out of *Vogue* and *Harper's Bazaar,* and favored Kleenex, and dressed her hair in a smart upsweep, and pinned silver flowers at her ears, and used My Sin perfume.

He loved to sit and watch her primp before the glass.

She didn't know whether she liked a little or a lot (a person could not always tell) the white woman married to a West Indian who lived in the third-floor kitchenette next Maud Martha's own. Through the day and night this woman, Eugena Banks, sang over and over again—varying the choruses, using what undoubtedly were her own improvisations, for they were very bad—the same popular song. Maud Martha had her own ideas about popular songs. "A popular song," thought she, "especially if it's one of the old, soft ones, is beautiful, sometimes, and seems to touch your mood exactly. But the touch is usually not full. You rise up with a popular song, but it isn't able to rise as high, once it has you started, as you are; by the time you've risen as high as it can take you you can't bear to stop, and you swell up and up and up till you're swelled to bursting. The popular music has long ago given up and left you."

This woman would come over, singing or humming her popular song, to see Maud Martha, wanting to know what special technique was to be used in dealing with a Negro man; a Negro man was a special type man; she knew that there should be, indeed, that there had to be, a special technique to be used with this type man, but what? And after all, there should be more than—than singing across the sock washing, the cornbread baking, the fish frying. No, she had not expected wealth, no—but he had seemed so exciting! so primitive!—life with a Negro man had looked, from the far side, like adventure—and the nights *were* good; but there were precious few of the nights, because he stayed away for days (though when he came back he was "very swell" and would hang up a picture or varnish a chair or let her make him some crêpes suzette, which she had always made so well).

Her own mother would not write to her; and she was, Mrs. Eugena Banks whined, beginning to wonder if it had not all been a mistake; could she not go back to Dayton? could she not begin again?

Then there was Clement Lewy, a little boy at the back, on the second floor.

Lewy life was not terrifically tossed. Saltless, rather. Or like an unmixed batter. Lumpy.

Little Clement's mother had grown listless after the desertion. She looked as though she had been scrubbed, up and down, on the washing board, doused from time to time in gray and noisome water. But little Clement looked alert, he looked happy, he was always spirited. He was in second grade. He did his work, and had always been promoted. At home he sang. He recited little poems. He told his mother little stories wound out of the air by himself. His mother glanced at him once in a while. She would have been proud of him if she had had the time.

She started toward her housemaid's work each morning at seven. She left a glass of milk and a bowl of dry cereal and a dish of prunes on the table, and set the alarm clock for eight. At eight little Clement punched off the alarm, stretched, got up, washed, dressed, combed, brushed, ate his breakfast. It was quiet in the apartment. He hurried off to school. At noon he returned from school, opened the door with his key. It was quiet in the apartment. He poured himself a second glass of milk, got more prunes, and ate a slice—"just one slice," his mother had cautioned—of bread and butter. He went back to school. At three o'clock he returned from school, opened the door with his key. It was quiet in the apartment. He got a couple of graham crackers out of the cookie can. He drew himself a glass of water. He changed his clothes. Then he went out to play, leaving behind him the two rooms. Leaving behind him the brass beds, the lamp with the faded silk tassel and frayed cord, the hooked oven door, the cracks in the walls and the quiet. As he played, he kept a lookout for his mother, who usually arrived at seven, or near that hour. When he saw her rounding the corner, his little face underwent a transformation. His eyes lashed into brightness, his lips opened suddenly and became a smile, and his eyebrows climbed toward his hairline in relief and joy.

He would run to his mother and almost throw his little body at her. "Here I am, mother! Here I am! Here I am!"

There was, or there had been, Richard—whose weekly earnings as a truck driver for a small beverage concern had dropped, slyly, from twenty-five, twenty-three, twenty-one, to sixteen, fifteen, twelve, while his weekly rent remained what it was (the family of five lived in one of the one-room apartments, a whole dollar cheaper than such a two-room as Paul and Maud Martha occupied); his family food and clothing bills had not dropped; and altogether it had been too much, the never having enough to buy Pabst or Ninety Proof for the boys, the being scared to death to offer a man a couple of cigarettes for fear your little supply, and with it your little weak-kneed nonchalance, might be exhausted before the appearance of your next pay envelope (pink, and designated elaborately on the outside, "Richard"), the coming back at night, every night, to a billowy diaper world, a wife with wild hair, twin brats screaming, and writhing, and wetting their crib, and a third brat, leaping on, from, and about chairs and table with repeated Hi-yo Silvers, and the sitting down to a meal never quite adequate, never quite—despite all your sacrifices, your inability to "treat" your friends, your shabby rags, your heartache. . . . It was altogether too much, so one night he had simply failed to come home.

There was an insane youth of twenty, twice released from Dunning. He had a smooth tan face, overlaid with oil. His name was Binnie. Or perhaps it was Bennie, or Benjamin. But his mother lovingly called him "Binnie." Binnie strode the halls, with huge eyes, direct and annoyed. He strode, and played "catch" with a broken watch, which was attached to a long string wound around his left arm. There was no annoyance in his eyes when he spoke to Maud Martha, though, and none in his nice voice. He was very fond of Maud Martha. Once, when she answered a rap on the door, there he was, and he pushed in before she could open her mouth. He had on a new belt, he said. "My Uncle John gave it to me," he said. "So my pants won't fall down." He walked about the apartment, after closing the door with a careful sneer. He touched things. He pulled a petal from a pink rose with savage anger, then kissed it with a tenderness that was more terrible than the anger; briskly he rapped on the table, turned suddenly to stare at her, to see if she approved of what he was doing—she smiled uncertainly; he saw the big bed, fingered it, sat on it, got up, kicked it. He opened a dresser drawer, took out a ruler. "This is ni-ice—but I won't take it" (with firm decision, noble virtue). "I'll put it back." He spoke of his aunt, his Uncle John's wife Octavia. "She's ni-ice—you know, she can even call me, and I don't even get mad." With another careful sneer, he opened the door. He went out.

Mrs. Teenie Thompson. Fifty-three; and pepper whenever she talked of the North Shore people who had employed her as housemaid for ten years. "She went to huggin' and kissin' of me—course I got to receive it—I got to work for 'em. But they think they got me thinkin' they love me. Then I'm supposed to kill my silly self slavin' for 'em. To be worthy of their love. These old whi' folks. They jive you, honey. Well, I jive 'em just like they jive me. They can't beat me jivin'. They'll have to jive much, to come anywhere *near* my mark in jivin'."

About one of the one-roomers, a little light woman flitted. She was thin and looked ill. Her hair, which was long and of a strangely flat blackness, hung absolutely still, no matter how much its mistress moved. If anyone passed her usually open door, she would nod cheerily, but she rarely spoke. Chiefly you would see her flitting, in a faded blue rayon housecoat, touching this, picking up that, adjusting, arranging, posing prettily. She was Mrs. Whitestripe. Mr. Whitestripe was a dark and dapper young man of medium height, with a small soot-smear of a mustache. The Whitestripes were the happiest couple Maud Martha had ever met. They were soft-spoken, kind to each other, were worried about each other. "Now you watch that cough now, Coopie!" For that was what she called him. "Here, take this Rem, here, take this lemon juice." "You wrap up good, now, you put on that scarf, Coo!" For that was what he called her. Or (rushing out of the door in his undershirt, one shoe off) "Did I hear you stumble down there, Coo? Did I hear you hurt your knee?" Often, visiting them, you were embarrassed, because it was obvious that you were interrupting the progress of a truly great love; even as you conversed, there they would be, kissing or patting each other, or gazing into each other' eyes. Most fitting was it that adjacent to their "domicile" was the balcony of the building. Unfortunately, it was about two inches wide. Three pressures of a firm foot, and the little balcony would crumble downward to mingle with other dust. The Whitestripes never sat on it, but Maud Martha had no doubt that often on summer evenings they would open the flimsy "French" door, and stand there gazing out, thinking of what little they knew about Romeo and Juliet, their arms about each other.

"It is such a beautiful story," sighed Maud Martha once, to Paul.

"What is?"

"The love story of the Whitestripes."

"Well, I'm no 'Coopie' Whitestripe," Paul had observed, sharply, "so you can stop mooning. I'll never be a 'Coopie' Whitestripe."

"No," agreed Maud Martha. "No, you never will."

The one-roomer next the Whitestripes was occupied by Maryginia Washington, a maiden of sixty-eight, or sixty-nine, or seventy, a becrutched, gnarled, bleached lemon with smartly bobbed white hair; who claimed, and proudly, to be an "indirect" descendant of the first President of the United States; who loathed the darker members of her race but did rather enjoy playing the *grande dame,* a hobbling, denture-clacking version, for their benefit, while they played, at least in her imagination, Topsys—and did rather enjoy advising them, from time to time, to apply lightening creams to the horror of their flesh—"because they ain't no sense in lookin' any worser'n you have to, is they, dearie?"

In the fifth section, on the third floor, lived a Woman of Breeding. Her name was Josephine Snow. She was too much of a Woman of Breeding to allow the title "Madame" to vulgarize her name, but certain inhabitants of the building had all they could do to keep from calling her

"Madame Snow," and eventually they relaxed, and called her that as a matter of course, behind her back.

Madame Snow was the color of soured milk, about sixty, and very superior to her surroundings —although she was not a Maryginia Washington. She had some sort of mysterious income, for although she had lived for seven years in "Gappington Arms" (the name given the building by the tenants, in dubious honor of the autocratic lady owner) no one had ever seen her go out to work. She rarely went anywhere. She went to church no more than once a month, and she sent little Clement Lewy and other children in the building to the store. She maintained a standard rate of pay; no matter how far the errand runner had to go, nor how heavily-loaded he was to be upon his return, she paid exactly five cents. It is hardly necessary to add that the identity of her runner was seldom the same for two days straight, and that a runner had to be poverty-stricken indeed before he searched among the paper nameplates downstairs and finally rang, with a disgruntled scowl, the bell of Miss Josephine Alberta Snow, Apt. 3E, who, actually, had been graduated from Fisk University.

What the source or size of Josephine's income was nobody knew. Her one-room apartment, although furnished with the same type of scarred brass bed and scratched dresser with which the other apartments were favored (for all her seven years), had received rich touches from her cultured hands. Her walls were hung with tapestry, strange pictures, china and illuminated poems. She had "lived well," as these things declared, and it was evident that she meant to go on "living well," Gappington Arms or no Gappington Arms.

This lady did the honors of the teacup and cookie crock each afternoon, with or without company. She would spread a large stool with a square of lace, deck it with a low bowl of artificial flowers, a teacup or teacups, the pot of tea, sugar, cream and lemon, and the odd-shaped crock of sweet crackers.

On indoor weekdays she wore always the same

dress—a black sateen thing that fell to her ankles and rose to her very chin. On the Sundays she condescended to go to church, she wore a pink lace, winter and summer, which likewise embraced her from ankle to chin. She charmed the neighborhood with that latter get-up, too, on those summer afternoons when the heat drove her down from her third-floor quarters to the little porch, with its one chair. There she would sit, frightening everyone, panting, fanning, and glaring at old Mr. Neville, the caretaker's eighty-two-year-old father, if he came out and so much as dared to look, with an eyeful of timid covetousness, at the single porch chair over which her bottom flowed (for she was a large lady). Then there was nothing for poor old Mr. Neville to do but sit silently on the hard stone steps—split, and crawling with ants and worse—chew his tobacco, glance peculiarly from time to time at that large pink lady, that pink and yellow lady, fanning indignantly at him.

As for the other tenants, they did not know what to say to Miss Snow after they had exchanged the time of day with her. Some few had attempted the tossing of sallies her way, centered in politics, the current murders, or homely philosophy, wanting to draw her out. But they very soon saw they would have to leave off all that, because it was too easy to draw her out. She would come out so far as to almost knock them down. She had a tremendous impatience with other people's ideas—unless those happened to be exactly like hers; even then, often as not, she gave hurried, almost angry, affirmative, and flew on to emphatic illuminations of her own. Then she would settle back in her chair, nod briskly a few times, as if to say, "Now! Now we are finished with it." What could be done? What was there further to be said?

24

an encounter

THEY went to the campus Jungly Hovel, a reedy-boothed place. Inside, before you saw anything, really, you got this impression of straw and reed. There were vendor outlets in the booths, and it could be observed what a struggle the management had had, trying to settle on something that was not out-and-out low, and that yet was not out-and-out highborn. In a weak moment someone had included Borden's Boogie Hoogie Woogie.

Maud Martha had gone to hear the newest

young Negro author speak, at Mandel Hall on the University campus, and whom had she run into, coming out, but David McKemster. Outside, David McKemster had been talking seriously with a tall, dignified old man. When he saw her, he gravely nodded. He gravely waved. She decided to wait for him, not knowing whether that would be agreeable to him or not. After all, this was the University world, this was his element. Perhaps he would feel she did not belong here, perhaps he would be cold to her.

He certainly was cold to her. Free of the dignified old man, he joined her, walked with her down Fifty-ninth Street, past the studious gray buildings, west toward Cottage Grove. He yawned heartily at every sixth or seventh step.

"I'll put you on a streetcar," he said. "God, I'm tired."

Then nothing more was said by him, or by her—till they met a young white couple, going east. David's face lit up. These were his good, good friends. He introduced them as such to Maud

Martha. Had they known about the panel discussion? No, they had not. Tell him, when had they seen Mary, Mary Ehreburg? Say, he had seen Metzger Freestone tonight. Ole Metzger. (He lit a cigarette.) Say, he had had dinner with the Beefy Godwins and Jane Wather this evening. Say, what were they doing tomorrow night? Well, what about going to the Adamses' tomorrow night? (He took excited but carefully sophisticated puffs.) Yes, they would go to the Adamses' tomorrow night. They would get Dora, and all go to the Adamses'. Say, how about going to Power's for a beer, tonight, if they had nothing else to do? Here he glanced at his companion—how to dispose of her! Well, no "how" about it, the disposal would have to be made. But first he had better buy her a coffee. That would pacify her. "Power'll still be up—prob'ly spr*awl*ing on that white rug of his, with Parrington in front of 'im," laughed David. It was, Maud Martha observed, one of the conceits of David McKemster that he did not have to use impeccable English all the time. Sometimes it was permissible to make careful slips. These must be, however, when possible, sandwiched in between thick hunks of the most rational, particularistic, critical, and intellectually aloof discourse. "But first let's go to the Jungly Hovel and have coffee with Mrs. Phillips," said David McKemster.

So off to the Jungly Hovel. They went into one of the booths and ordered.

The strange young man's face was pleasant when it smiled; the jaw was a little forward; Maud Martha was reminded of Pat O'Brien, the movie star. He kept looking at her; when he looked at her his eyes were somewhat agape; "Well!" they seemed to exclaim—"Well! and what have we here!" The girl, who was his fiancée, it turned out—"Stickie"—had soft pink coloring, summer-blue eyes, was attractive. She had, her soft pink notwithstanding, that brisk, thriving, noisy, "oh-so-American" type of attractiveness. She was confidential, she communicated everything except herself, which was precisely the thing her eyes, her words, her nods, her suddenly whipped-off laughs assured you she *was* communicating. She leaned healthily across the table; her long, lovely dark hair swung at you; her bangs came right out to meet you, and her face and forefinger did too (she emphasized, robustly, some point). But herself stayed stuck to the back of her seat, and was shrewd, and "took in," and contemplated, not quite warmly, everything.

"And there was this young—man. Twenty-one or two years old, wasn't he, Maudie?" David looked down at his guest. When they sat, their heights were equal, for his length was in the legs. But he thought he was looking down at her, and she was very willing to concede that that was what he was doing, for the immediate effect of the look was to make her sit straight as a stick. "Really quite, really most a*maz*ing. Didn't you think, Maudie? Has written a book. Seems well-read chap, seems to know a lot about—a lot about—"

"Everything," supplied Maud Martha furiously.

"Well—yes." His brows gathered. He stabbed "Stickie" with a well-made gaze of seriousness, sober economy, doubt—mixed. "PRESENT things," he emphasized sharply. "He's very impressed by, he's all adither about—current plays in New York —Kafka. *That* sawt of thing," he ended. His "sawt" was not sarcastic. Our position is hardly challenged, it implied. We are still on top of the wave, it implied. We, who know about Aristotle, Plato, who weave words like anachronism, transcendentalist, cosmos, metaphysical, corollary, integer, monarchical, into our breakfast speech as a matter of course—

"And he disdains the universities!"

"Is he in school?" asked "Stickie," leaning: on the answer to that would depend—so much.

"Oh, no," David assured her, smiling. "He was pretty forceful on that point. There is nothing in the schools for *him,* he has decided. What are degrees, he asks contemptously." You see? David McKemster implied. This upstart, this, this brazen emissary, this rash representative from the ranks of the intellectual *nouveau riche.* So he was brilliant. So he could outchatter me. So intellectuality was his oyster. So he has kicked—not Parrington—but Joyce, maybe, around like a football. But he is not rooted in Aristotle, in Plato, in Aeschylus, in Epictetus. In all those Goddamn Greeks. As we are. Aloud, David skirted some of this—"Aristotle," he said, "is probably Greek to him." "Stickie" laughed quickly, stopped. Pat O'Brien smiled lazily; leered.

The waitress brought coffee, four lumps of sugar wrapped in pink paper, hot mince pie.

25

the self-solace

SONIA JOHNSON got together her towels and soap. She scrubbed out her bowls. She mixed her water.

Maud Martha, waiting, was quiet. It was pleasant to let her mind go blank. And here in the beauty shop that was not a difficult thing to do. For the perfumes in the great jars, to be sold for twelve dollars and fifty cents an ounce and one dollar a dram, or seven dollars and fifty cents an ounce and one dollar a dram, the calendars, the bright signs extolling the virtues of Lily cologne

(Made by the Management), the limp lengths of detached human hair, the pile of back-number *Vogues* and *Bazaars,* the earrings and clasps and beaded bags, white blouses—the "side line"—these things did not force themselves into the mind and make a disturbance there. One was and was not aware of them. Could sit here and think, or not think, of problems. Think, or not. One did not have to, if one wished not.

"If she burns me today—if she yanks at my hair —if she calls me sweetheart or dahlin'—"

Sonia Johnson parted the hangings that divided her reception room from her workrooms. "Come on back, baby doll."

But just then the bell tinkled, and in pushed a young white woman, wearing a Persian lamb coat, and a Persian lamb cap with black satin ribbon swirled capably in a soft knot at the back.

"Yes," thought Maud Martha, "it's legitimate. It's November. It's not cold, but it's cool. You can wear your new fur now and not be laughed at by too many people."

The young white woman introduced herself to Mrs. Johnson as Miss Ingram, and said that she had new toilet waters, a make-up base that was so good it was "practically impossible," and a new lipstick.

"No make-up bases," said Sonia. "And no toilet water. We create our own."

"This new lipstick, this new shade," Miss Ingram said, taking it out of a smart little black bag, "is just the thing for your customers. For their dark complexions."

Sonia Johnson looked interested. She always put herself out to be kind and polite to these white salesmen and saleswomen. Some beauticians were brusque. They were almost insulting. They were glad to have the whites at their mercy, if only for a few moments. They made them crawl. Then they applied the whiplash. Then they sent the poor creatures off—with no orders. Then they laughed and laughed and laughed, a terrible laughter. But Sonia Johnson was not that way. She liked to be kind and polite. She liked to be merciful. She did not like to take advantage of her power. Indeed, she felt it was better to strain, to bend far back, to spice one's listening with the smooth smile, the quick and attentive nod, the well-timed "sure" or "uh-huh." She was against this eye-for-eye-tooth-for-tooth stuff.

Maud Martha looked at Miss Ingram's beautiful legs, wondered where she got the sheer stockings that looked like bare flesh at the same time that they did not, wondered if Miss Ingram knew that in the "Negro group" there were complexions whiter than her own, and other complexions, brown, tan, yellow, cream, which could not take a dark lipstick and keep their poise. Maud Martha picked up an ancient *Vogue,* turned the pages.

"What's the lipstick's name?" Sonia Johnson asked.

"Black Beauty," Miss Ingram said, with firm-lipped determination. "You won't regret adding it to your side line, I assure you, Madam."

"What's it sell for?"

"A dollar and a half. Let me leave you—say,

ten—and in a week I'll come back and find them all gone, and you'll be here clamoring for more, I know you will. I'll leave ten."

"Well. Okay."

"That's fine, Madam. Now, I'll write down your name and address—"

Sonia rattled them off for her. Miss Ingram wrote them down. Then she closed her case.

"Now, I'll take just five dollars. Isn't that reasonable? You don't pay the rest till they're all sold. Oh, I know you're going to be just terribly pleased. And your customers too, Mrs. Johnson."

Sonia opened her cash drawer and took out five dollars for Miss Ingram. Miss Ingram brightened. The deal was closed. She pushed back a puff of straw-colored hair that had slipped from under her Persian lamb cap and fallen over the faint rose of her cheek.

"I'm mighty glad," she confided, "that the cold weather is in. I love the cold. It was awful, walking the streets in that nasty old August weather. And even September was rather close this year, didn't you think?"

Sonia agreed. "Sure was."

"People," confided Miss Ingram, "think this is a snap job. It ain't. I work like a nigger to make a few pennies. A few lousy pennies."

Maud Martha's head shot up. She did not look at Miss Ingram. She stared intently at Sonia Johnson. Sonia Johnson's sympathetic smile remained. Her eyes turned, as if magnetized, toward Maud Martha; but she forced her smile to stay on. Maud Martha went back to *Vogue*. "For," she thought, "I must have been mistaken. I was afraid I heard that woman say 'nigger.' Apparently not. Because of course Mrs. Johnson wouldn't let her get away with it. In her own shop." Maud Martha closed *Vogue*. She began to consider what she herself might have said, had she been Sonia Johnson, and had the woman really said "nigger." "I wouldn't curse. I wouldn't holler. I'll bet Mrs. Johnson would do both those things. And I could understand her wanting to, all right. I would be gentle in a cold way. I would give her, not a return insult—directly, at any rate!—but information. I would get it across to her that—" Maud Martha stretched. "But I wouldn't insult her." Maud Martha began to take the hairpins out of her hair. "I'm glad, though, that she didn't say it. She's pretty and pleasant. If she had said it, I would feel all strained and tied up inside, and I would feel that it was my duty to help Mrs. Johnson get it settled, to help clear it up in some way. I'm too relaxed to fight today. Sometimes fighting is interesting. Today, it would have been just plain old ugly duty."

"Well, I wish you success with Black Beauty," Miss Ingram said, smiling in a tired manner, as she buttoned the top button of her Persian lamb. She walked quickly out of the door. The little bell tinkled charmingly.

Sonia Johnson looked at her customer with thoughtful narrowed eyes. She walked over, dragged a chair up close. She sat. She began to speak in a dull level tone.

"You know, why I didn't catch her up on that,

is—our people is got to stop feeling so sensitive about these words like 'nigger' and such. I often think about this, and how these words like 'nigger' don't mean to some of these here white people what our people *think* they mean. Now, 'nigger,' for instance, means to them something bad, or slavey-like, or low. They don't mean anything against me. I'm a Negro, not a 'nigger.' Now, a white man can be a 'nigger,' according to their meaning for the word, just like a colored man can. So why should I go getting all stepped up about a thing like that? Our people is got to stop getting all stepped up about every little thing, especially when it don't amount to nothing. . . ."

"You mean to say," Maud Martha broke in, "that that woman really did say 'nigger'?"

"Oh, yes, she said it, all right, but like I'm telling—"

"Well! At first, I thought she said it, but then I decided I must have been mistaken, because you weren't getting after her."

"Now that's what I'm trying to explain to you,

dearie. Sure, I could have got all hot and bothered, and told her to clear out of here, or cussed her daddy, or something like that. But what would be the point, when, like I say, that word 'nigger' can mean one of them just as fast as one of us, and in fact it don't mean us, and in fact we're just too sensitive and all? What would be the point? Why make enemies? Why go getting all hot and bothered all the time?"

Maud Martha stared steadily into Sonia Johnson's irises. She said nothing. She kept on staring into Sonia Johnson's irises.

26

Maud Martha's tumor

AS she bent over Paulette, she felt a peculiar pain in her middle, at the right. She touched the spot. There it was. A knot, hard, manipulable, the proscription of her doom.

At first, she could only be weak (as the pain grew sharper and sharper). Then she was aware of creeping fear; fear of the operating table, the glaring instruments, the cold-faced nurses, the relentlessly submerging ether, the chokeful awakening, the pain, the ensuing cancer, the ensuing death.

Then she thought of her life. Decent childhood, happy Christmases; some shreds of romance, a marriage, pregnancy and the giving birth, her growing child, her experiments in sewing, her books, her conversations with her friends and enemies.

"It hasn't been bad," she thought.

"It's been interesting," she thought, as she put Paulette in the care of Mrs. Maxawanda Barksdale and departed for the doctor's.

She looked at the trees, she looked at the grass, she looked at the faces of the passers-by. It had been interesting, it had been rather good, and it was still rather good. But really, she was ready. Since the time had come, she was ready. Paulette would miss her for a long time, Paul for less, but really, their sorrow was their business, not hers. Her business was to descend into the deep cool, the salving dark, to be alike indifferent to the good and the not-good.

Maud Martha's tumor

"And what," asked Dr. Williams, "did you do yesterday that was out of line with your regular routine?" He mashed her here, tapped there.

She remembered.

"Why, I was doing the bends."

"Doing—"

"The bends. Exercising. With variations. I lay on the bed, also, and keeping my upper part absolutely still, I raised my legs up, then lowered them, twenty times."

"Is this a nightly custom of yours?"

"No. Last night was the first time I had done it since before my little girl was born."

"Three dollars, please."

"You mean—I'm not going to die."

She bounced down the long flight of tin-edged stairs, was shortly claimed by the population, which seemed proud to have her back. An old woman, bent, shriveled, smiled sweetly at her.

She was already on South Park. She jumped in a jitney and went home.

27

Paul in the 011 Club

THE 011 Club did not like it so much, your buying only a beer. . . .

Do you want to get into the war? Maud Martha "thought at" Paul, as, over their wine, she watched his eye-light take leave of her. To get into the war, perhaps. To be mixed up in peculiar, hooped adventure, adventure dominant, entire, ablaze with bunched and fidgeting color, pageantry, thrilling with the threat of danger—through which he would come without so much as a bruised ankle.

Paul in the 011 Club

The baby was getting darker all the time! She knew that he was tired of his wife, tired of his living quarters, tired of working at Sam's, tired of his two suits.

He is ever so tired, she thought.

He had no money, no car, no clothes, and he had not been put up for membership in the Foxy Cats Club.

Something should happen. He was not on show. She knew that he believed he had been born to invade, to occur, to confront, to inspire the flapping of flags, to panic people. To wear, but carelessly, a crown. What could give him his chance, illuminate his gold?—be a happening?

She looked about, about at these, the people he would like to impress. The real people. It was Sunday afternoon and they were dressed in their best. It was May, and for hats the women wore gardens and birds. They wore tight-fitting prints, or flounced satin, or large-flowered silk under the coats they could not afford but bought anyhow. Their hair was intricately curled, or it was sedately marcelled. Some of it was hennaed. Their escorts were in broad-shouldered suits, and sported dapper handkerchiefs. Their hair was either slicked back or very close-cut. All spoke in subdued tones. There were no roughnecks here. These people knew what whiskies were good, what wine was "the thing" with this food, that food, what places to go, how to dance, how to smoke, how much stress to put on love, how to dress, when to curse, and did not indulge (for the most part) in homosexuality but could discuss it without eagerness, distaste, curiosity—without anything but ennui. These, in her husband's opinion, were the real people. And this was the real place. The manner of the waitresses toward the patrons, by unspoken agreement, was just this side of insulting. They seemed to have something to prove. They wanted you to know, to be *sure* that they were as good as you were and maybe a lot better. They did not want you to be misled by the fact that on a Sunday afternoon, instead of silk and little foxes, they wore white uniforms and carried trays and picked up (rapidly) tips.

A flame-colored light flooded the ceiling in the dining foyer. (But there was a blue-red-purple note in the bar.) On the east wall of the dining foyer, painted against a white background, was an unclothed lady, with a careless bob, challenging nipples, teeth-revealing smile; her arms were lifted, to call attention to "all"—and she was standing behind a few huge leaves of sleepy color and amazing design. On the south wall was painted one of those tropical ladies clad in carefully careless sarong, and bearing upon her head with great ease and glee a platter of fruit—apples, spiky pineapple, bananas. . . .

She watched the little dreams of smoke as they spiraled about his hand, and she thought about happenings. She was afraid to suggest to him that, to most people, nothing at all "happens." That most people merely live from day to day until they die. That, after he had been dead a year, doubtless fewer than five people would think of him oftener than once a year. That there might even come a year when no one on earth would think of him at all.

28

brotherly love

MAUD MARTHA was fighting with a chicken. The nasty, nasty mess. It had been given a bitter slit with the bread knife and the bread knife had been biting in that vomit-looking interior for almost five minutes without being able to detach certain resolute parts from their walls. The bread knife had it all to do, as Maud Martha had no intention of putting her hand in there. Another hack—another hack—STUFF! Splat in her eye. She leaped at the faucet.

She thought she had praise coming to her. She was doing this job with less stomach-curving than ever before. She thought of the times before the war, when there were more chickens than people wanting to buy them, and butchers were happy to clean them, and even cut them up. None of that now. In those happy, happy days—if she had opened up a chicken and seen it all unsightly like this, and smelled it all smelly, she would have scooped up the whole batch of slop and rushed it to the garbage can. Now meat was jewelry and she was practically out of Red Points. You were lucky to find a chicken. She had to be as brave as she could.

People could do this! people could cut a chicken open, take out the mess, with bare hands or a bread knife, pour water in, as in a bag, pour water out, shake the corpse by neck or by legs, free the straggles of water. Could feel that insinuating slipping bone, survey that soft, that headless death. The *faint*hearted could do it. But if the chicken were a man!—cold man with no head or feet and with all the little feath—er, hairs to be pulled, and the intestines loosened and beginning to ooze out, and the gizzard yet to be grabbed and the stench beginning to rise! And yet the chicken was a sort of person, a respectable individual, with its own kind of dignity. The difference was in the knowing. What was unreal to you, you could deal with violently. If chickens were ever to be safe, people would have to live with them, and know them, see them loving their children, finishing the evening meal, arranging jealousy.

When the animal was ready for the oven Maud Martha smacked her lips at the thought of her meal.

29

millinery

"LOOKS lovely on you," said the manager. "Makes you look—" What? Beautiful? Charming? Glamorous? Oh no, oh no, she could not stoop to the usual lies; not today; her coffee had been too strong, had not set right; and there had been another fight at home, for her daughter continued to insist on gallivanting about with that Greek—a Greek!—not even a Jew, which, though revolting enough, was at least becoming fashionable, was "timely." Oh, not today would she cater to these nigger women who tried on every hat in her shop, who used no telling what concoctions of smelly grease on the heads that integrity, straightforwardness, courage, would certainly have kept kinky. She started again—"Makes you look—" She stopped.

"How much is the hat?" Maud Martha asked.

"Seven ninety-nine."

Maud Martha rose, went to the door.

"Wait, wait," called the hat woman, hurrying after her. She smiled at Maud Martha. When she looked at Maud Martha, it was as if God looked; it was as if—

"Now just how much, Madam, had you thought you would prefer to pay?"

"Not a cent over five."

"Five? Five, dearie? You expect to buy a hat like this for five dollars? This, this straw that you can't even get any more and which I showed you only because you looked like a lady of taste who could appreciate a good value?"

"Well," said Maud Martha, "thank you." She opened the door.

"Wait, wait," shrieked the hat woman. Good-naturedly, the escaping customer hesitated again. "Just a moment," ordered the hat woman coldly. "I'll speak to the—to the owner. He might be willing to make some slight reduction, since you're an old customer. I remember you. You've been in here several times, haven't you?"

"I've never been in the store before." The woman rushed off as if she had heard nothing. She rushed off to consult with the owner. She rushed off to appeal to the boxes in the back room.

Presently the hat woman returned.

"Well. The owner says it'll be a crying shame, but seeing as how you're such an old customer he'll make a reduction. He'll let you have it for five. Plus tax, of course!" she added chummily; they had, always, more appreciation when, after one of these "reductions," you added that.

"I've decided against the hat."

"What? Why, you told— But, you said—"

millinery

Maud Martha went out, tenderly closed the door.

"Black—oh, black—" said the hat woman to her hats—which, on the slender stands, shone pink and blue and white and lavender, showed off their tassels, their sleek satin ribbons, their veils, their flower coquettes.

30

at the Burns-Coopers'

IT was a little red and white and black woman who appeared in the doorway of the beautiful house in Winnetka.

About, thought Maud Martha, thirty-four.

"I'm Mrs. Burns-Cooper," said the woman, "and after this, well, it's all right this time, because it's your first time, but after this time always use the back entrance."

There is a pear in my icebox, and one end of rye

bread. Except for three Irish potatoes and a cup of flour and the empty Christmas boxes, there is absolutely nothing on my shelf. My husband is laid off. There is newspaper on my kitchen table instead of oilcloth. I can't find a filing job in a hurry. I'll smile at Mrs. Burns-Cooper and hate her just some.

"First, you have the beds to make," said Mrs. Burns-Cooper. "You either change the sheets or air the old ones for ten minutes. I'll tell you about the changing when the time comes. It isn't any special day. You are to pull my sheets, and pat and pat and pull till all's tight and smooth. Then shake the pillows into the slips, carefully. Then punch them in the middle.

"Next, there is the washing of the midnight snack dishes. Next, there is the scrubbing. Now, I know that your other ladies have probably wanted their floors scrubbed after dinner. I'm different. I like to enjoy a bright clean floor all the day. You can just freshen it up a little before you leave in the evening, if it needs a few more touches. Another thing. I disapprove of mops. You can do a better job on your knees.

"Next is dusting. Next is vacuuming—that's for Tuesdays and Fridays. On Wednesdays, ironing and silver cleaning.

"Now about cooking. You're very fortunate in that here you have only the evening meal to prepare. Neither of us has breakfast, and I always step out for lunch. Isn't that lucky?"

"It's quite a kitchen, isn't it?" Maud Martha observed. "I mean, big."

Mrs. Burns-Cooper's brows raced up in amazement.

"Really? I hadn't thought so. I'll bet"—she twinkled indulgently—"you're comparing it to your *own* little kitchen." And why do that, her light eyes laughed. Why talk of beautiful mountains and grains of alley sand in the same breath?

"Once," mused Mrs. Burns-Cooper, "I had a girl who botched up the kitchen. Made a botch out of it. But all I had to do was just sort of cock my head and say, 'Now, now, Albertine!' Her name was Albertine. Then she'd giggle and scrub and scrub and she was *so* sorry about trying to take advantage."

It was while Maud Martha was peeling potatoes for dinner that Mrs. Burns-Cooper laid herself out to prove that she was not a snob. Then it was that Mrs. Burns-Cooper came out to the kitchen and, sitting, talked and talked at Maud Martha. In my college days. At the time of my debut. The imported lace on my lingerie. My brother's rich wife's Stradivarius. When I was in Madrid. The charm of the Nile. Cost fifty dollars. Cost one hundred dollars. Cost one thousand dollars. Shall I mention, considered Maud Martha, my own social triumphs, my own education, my travels to Gary and Milwaukee and Columbus, Ohio? Shall I mention my collection of fancy pink satin bras? She decided against it. She went on listening, in silence, to the confidences until the arrival of the lady's mother-in-law (large-eyed, strong, with hair of a mighty white, and with an eloquent, angry bosom). Then the junior Burns-Cooper was very much the mistress, was stiff, cool, authoritative.

There was no introduction, but the elder Burns-Cooper boomed, "Those potato parings are entirely too thick!"

The two of them, richly dressed, and each with that health in the face that bespeaks, or seems to bespeak, much milk drinking from earliest childhood, looked at Maud Martha. There was no remonstrance; no firing! They just looked. But for the first time, she understood what Paul endured daily. For so—she could gather from a Paul-word here, a Paul-curse there—his Boss! when, squared, upright, terribly upright, superior to the President, commander of the world, he wished to underline Paul's lacks, to indicate soft shock, controlled incredulity. As his boss looked at Paul, so these people looked at her. As though she were a child, a ridiculous one, and one that ought to be given a little shaking, except that shaking was—not quite the thing, would not quite do. One held up one's finger (if one did anything), cocked one's head, was arch. As in the old song, one hinted, "Tut tut! now now! come come!" Metal rose, all built, in one's eye.

I'll never come back, Maud Martha assured herself, when she hung up her apron at eight in the evening. She knew Mrs. Burns-Cooper would be puzzled. The wages were very good. Indeed, what could be said in explanation? Perhaps that the hours were long. I couldn't explain *my* explanation, she thought.

One walked out from that almost perfect wall, spitting at the firing squad. What difference did it make whether the firing squad understood or did not understand the manner of one's retaliation or why one had to retaliate?

Why, one was a human being. One wore clean nightgowns. One loved one's baby. One drank cocoa by the fire—or the gas range—come the evening, in the wintertime.

31

on Thirty-fourth Street

MAUD MARTHA went east on Thirty-fourth Street, headed for Cottage Grove. It was August, and Thirty-fourth Street was all in bloom. The blooms, in their undershirts, sundresses and diapers, were hanging over porches and fence stiles and strollers, and were even bringing chairs out to the rims of the sidewalks.

At the corner of Thirty-fourth and Cottage Grove, a middle-aged blind man on a three-legged stool picked at a scarred guitar. The five or six patched and middle-aged men around him sang in husky, low tones, which carried the higher tone—ungarnished, insistent, at once a question and an answer—of the instrument.

Those men were going no further—and had gone nowhere. Tragedy.

She considered that word. On the whole, she felt, life was more comedy than tragedy. Nearly everything that happened had its comic element, not too well buried, either. Sooner or later one could find something to laugh at in almost every situation. That was what, in the last analysis, could keep folks from going mad. The truth was, if you got a good Tragedy out of a lifetime, one good, ripping tragedy, thorough, unridiculous, bottom-scraping, *not* the issue of human stupidity, you were doing, she thought, very well, you were doing well.

32

Mother comes to call

MAMA came, bringing two oranges, nine pecans, a Hershey bar and a pear.

Mama explained that one of the oranges was for Maud Martha, one was for Paulette. The Hershey bar was for Paulette. The pear was for Maud Martha, for it was not, Mama said, a very good pear. Four of the pecans were for Maud Martha, four were for Paulette, one was for Paul.

Maud Martha spread her little second-hand table—a wide tin band was wound beneath the top, for strength—with her finest wedding gift, a really good white luncheon cloth. She brought out white coffee cups and saucers, sugar, milk, and a little pink pot of cocoa. She brought a plate of frosted gingerbread. Mother and daughter sat down to Tea.

"And how is Helen? I haven't seen her in two weeks. When I'm over there to see you, she's always out."

"Helen doesn't like to come here much," said Mama, nodding her head over the gingerbread. "Not enough cinnamon in this but very good. She says it sort of depresses her. She wants you to have more things."

"I like nutmeg better than cinnamon. I have a lot of things. I have more than she has. I have a husband, a nice little girl, and a clean home of my own."

"A kitchenette of your own," corrected Mama, "without even a private bathroom. I think Paul could do a little better, Maud Martha."

"It's hard to find even a kitchenette."

"Nothing beats a trial but a failure. Helen thinks she's going to marry Doctor Williams."

"Our own family doctor. Not our own family doctor!"

"She says her mind's about made up."

"But he's over fifty years old."

"She says he's steady, not like the young ones she knows, and kind, and will give her a decent home."

"And what do you say?"

"I say, it's a hard cold world and a woman had better do all she can to help herself get along as long as what she does is honest. It isn't as if she didn't like Doctor Williams."

"She always did, yes. Ever since we were children, and he used to bring her licorice sticks, and forgot to bring any to me, except very seldom."

"It isn't as if she merely sold herself. She'll try to make him happy, I'm sure. Helen was always a good girl. And in any marriage, the honeymoon is soon over."

"What does Papa say?"

"He's thinking of changing doctors."

"It hasn't been a hard cold world for you, Mama. You've been very lucky. You've had a faithful, homecoming husband, who bought you a house, not the best house in town, but a house. You have, most of the time, plenty to eat, you have enough clothes so that you can always be clean. And you're strong as a horse."

"It certainly has been a hard season," said Belva Brown. "I don't know when we've had to burn so much coal in October before."

"I'm thinking of Helen."

"What about Helen, dear?"

"It's funny how some people are just charming, just pretty, and others, born of the same parents, are just not."

"You've always been wonderful, dear."

They looked at each other.

"I always say you make the best cocoa in the family."

"I'm never going to tell my secret."

"That girl down at the corner, next to the parsonage—you know?—is going to have another baby."

"The third? And not her husband's *either*?"

"Not her husband's either."

"Did Mrs. Whitfield get all right?"

"No, she'll have to have the operation."

33

tree leaves leaving trees

AIRPLANES and games and dolls and books and wagons and blackboards and boats and guns and bears and rabbits and pandas and ducks, and dogs and cats and gray elephants with black howdahs and rocking chairs and houses and play dishes and scooters and animal hassocks, and trains and trucks and yo-yos and telephones and balls and jeeps and jack-in-the-boxes and puzzles and rocking horses.

And Santa Claus.

Round, ripe, rosy,
As the stories said.
And white, it fluffed out from his chin,
It laughed about his head.

And there were the children. Many groups of them, for this was a big department store. Santa pushed out plump ho-ho-ho's! He patted the children's cheeks, and if a curl was golden and sleek enough he gave it a bit of a tug, and sometimes he gave its owner a bit of a hug. And the children's Christmas wants were almost torn out of them.

It was very merry and much as the children had dreamed.

Now came little Paulette. When the others had been taken care of. Her insides scampering like mice. And, leaving her eyeballs, diamonds and stars.

Santa Claus.

Suddenly she was shy.

Maud Martha smiled, gave her a tiny shove, spoke as much to Santa Claus as to her daughter.

"Go on. There he is. You've wanted to talk to him all this time. Go on. Tell Santa what you want for Christmas."

"No."

Another smile, another shove, with some impatience, with some severity in it. And Paulette was off.

"Hello!"

Santa Claus rubbed his palms together and looked vaguely out across the Toy Department.

He was unable to see either mother or child.

"I want," said Paulette, "a wagon, a doll, a big ball, a bear and a tricycle with a horn."

"Mister," said Maud Martha, "my little girl is talking to you."

Santa Claus's neck turned with hard slowness, carrying his unwilling face with it.

"Mister," said Maud Martha.

"And what—do you want for Christmas." No question mark at the end.

"I want a wagon, a doll, a bear, a big ball, and a tricycle with a horn."

Silence. Then, "Oh." Then, "Um-hm."

Santa Claus had taken care of Paulette.

"And some candy and some nuts and a seesaw and bow and arrow."

"Come on, baby."

"But I'm not through, Mama."

"Santa Claus is through, hon."

Outside, there was the wonderful snow, high and heavy, crusted with blue twinkles. The air was quiet.

"Certainly is a nice night," confided Mama.

"Why didn't Santa Claus like me?"

"Baby, of course he liked you."

"He didn't like me. Why didn't he like me?"

"It maybe seemed that way to you. He has a lot on his mind, of course."

"He liked the other children. He smiled at them and shook their hands."

"He maybe got tired of smiling. Sometimes even I get—"

"He didn't look at me, he didn't shake *my* hand."

"Listen, child. People don't have to kiss you to show they like you. Now you know Santa Claus liked you. What have I been telling you? Santa Claus loves every child, and on the night before Christmas he brings them swell presents. Don't you remember, when you told Santa Claus you wanted the ball and bear and tricycle and doll he said 'Um-hm'? That meant he's going to bring you all those. You watch and see. Christmas'll be here in a few days. You'll wake up Christmas morning and find them and then you'll know Santa Claus loved *you too.*"

Helen, she thought, would not have twitched, back there. Would not have yearned to jerk trimming scissors from purse and jab jab jab that evading eye. Would have gathered her fires, patted them, rolled them out, and blown on them. Because it really would not have made much difference to Helen. Paul would have twitched, twitched awfully, might have cursed, but after the first tough cough-up of rage would forget, or put off studious perusal indefinitely.

tree leaves leaving trees

She could neither resolve nor dismiss. There were these scraps of baffled hate in her, hate with no eyes, no smile and—this she especially regretted, called her hungriest lack—not much voice.

Furtively, she looked down at Paulette. Was Paulette believing her? Surely she was not going to begin to think tonight, to try to find out answers tonight. She hoped the little creature wasn't ready. She hoped there hadn't been enough for that. She wasn't up to coping with— Some other night, not tonight.

Feeling her mother's peep, Paulette turned her face upward. Maud Martha wanted to cry.

Keep her that land of blue!

Keep her those fairies, with witches always killed at the end, and Santa every winter's lord, kind, sheer being who never perspires, who never does or says a foolish or ineffective thing, who never looks grotesque, who never has occasion to pull the chain and flush the toilet.

34

back from the wars!

THERE was Peace, and her brother Harry was back from the wars, and well.

And it was such a beautiful day!

The weather was bidding her bon voyage.

She did not have to tip back the shade of her little window to know that outside it was bright, because the sunshine had broken through the dark green of that shade and was glorifying every bit of her room. And the air crawling in at the half-inch crack was like a feather, and it tickled her throat, it teased her lashes, it made her sit up in bed and stretch, and zip the dark green shade up to the very top of the window—and made her whisper, What, *what*, am I to do with all of this life?

And exactly what was one to do with it all? At a moment like this one was ready for anything, was not afraid of anything. If one were down in a dark cool valley one could stick arms out and presto! they would be wings cutting away at the higher layers of air. At a moment like this one could think even of death with a sharp exhilaration, feel that death was a part of life: that life was good and death would be good too.

Maud Martha, with her daughter, got out-of-doors.

She did not need information, or solace, or a guidebook, or a sermon—not in this sun!—not in this blue air!

. . . They "marched," they battled behind her brain—the men who had drunk beer with the best of them, the men with two arms off and two legs *back from the wars!*

off, the men with the parts of faces. Then her guts divided, then her eyes swam under frank mist.

And the Negro press (on whose front pages beamed the usual representations of womanly Beauty, pale and pompadoured) carried the stories of the latest of the Georgia and Mississippi lynchings. . . .

But the sun was shining, and some of the people in the world had been left alive, and it was doubtful whether the ridiculousness of man would ever completely succeed in destroying the world—or, in fact, the basic equanimity of the least and commonest flower: for would its kind not come up again in the spring? come up, if necessary, among, between, or out of—beastly inconvenient!—the smashed corpses lying in strict composure, in that hush infallible and sincere.

And was not this something to be thankful for?

And, in the meantime, while people did live they would be grand, would be glorious and brave, would have nimble hearts that would beat and beat. They would even get up nonsense, through wars, through divorce, through evictions and jiltings and taxes.

And, in the meantime, she was going to have another baby.

The weather was bidding her bon voyage.

The Bean Eaters

1960

In Honor of David Anderson Brooks, My Father

JULY 30, 1883–NOVEMBER 21, 1959

A dryness is upon the house
My father loved and tended.
Beyond his firm and sculptured door
His light and lease have ended.

He walks the valleys, now—replies
To sun and wind forever.
No more the cramping chamber's chill,
No more the hindering fever.

Now out upon the wide clean air
My father's soul revives,
All innocent of self-interest
And the fear that strikes and strives.

He who was Goodness, Gentleness,
And Dignity is free,
Translates to public Love
Old private charity.

The Explorer

Somehow to find a still spot in the noise
Was the frayed inner want, the winding, the frayed hope
Whose tatters he kept hunting through the din.
A satin peace somewhere.
A room of wily hush somewhere within.

So tipping down the scrambled halls he set
Vague hands on throbbing knobs. There were behind
Only spiraling, high human voices,
The scream of nervous affairs,
Wee griefs,
Grand griefs. And choices.

He feared most of all the choices, that cried to be taken.

There were no bourns.
There were no quiet rooms.

My Little 'Bout-town Gal

ROGER OF RHODES

My little 'bout-town gal has gone
'Bout town with powder and blue dye
On her pale lids and on her lips
Dye sits quite carminely.

I'm scarcely healthy-hearted or human.
What can I teach my cheated Woman?

My Tondeleyo, my black blonde
Will not be homing soon.
None shall secure her save the late the
Detective fingers of the moon.

Strong Men, Riding Horses

LESTER AFTER THE WESTERN

Strong Men, riding horses. In the West
On a range five hundred miles. A Thousand. Reaching
From dawn to sunset. Rested blue to orange.
From hope to crying. Except that Strong Men are
Desert-eyed. Except that Strong Men are
Pasted to stars already. Have their cars
Beneath them. Rentless, too. Too broad of chest
To shrink when the Rough Man hails. Too flailing
To redirect the Challenger, when the challenge
Nicks ; slams ; buttonholes. Too saddled.

I am not like that. I pay rent, am addled
By illegible landlords, run, if robbers call.

What mannerisms I present, employ,
Are camouflage, and what my mouths remark
To word-wall off that broadness of the dark
Is pitiful.
I am not brave at all.

The Bean Eaters

They eat beans mostly, this old yellow pair.
Dinner is a casual affair.
Plain chipware on a plain and creaking wood,
Tin flatware.

Two who are Mostly Good.
Two who have lived their day,
But keep on putting on their clothes
And putting things away.

And remembering . . .
Remembering, with twinklings and twinges,
As they lean over the beans in their rented back room that
is full of beads and receipts and dolls and cloths,
tobacco crumbs, vases and fringes.

We Real Cool

THE POOL PLAYERS.
SEVEN AT THE GOLDEN SHOVEL.

We real cool. We
Left school. We

Lurk late. We
Strike straight. We

Sing sin. We
Thin gin. We

Jazz June. We
Die soon.

Old Mary

My last defense
Is the present tense.

It little hurts me now to know
I shall not go

Cathedral-hunting in Spain
Nor cherrying in Michigan or Maine.

A Bronzeville Mother Loiters in Mississippi. Meanwhile, a Mississippi Mother Burns Bacon

From the first it had been like a
Ballad. It had the beat inevitable. It had the blood.
A wildness cut up, and tied in little bunches,
Like the four-line stanzas of the ballads she had never quite
Understood — the ballads they had set her to, in school.

Herself: the milk-white maid, the "maid mild"
Of the ballad. Pursued
By the Dark Villain. Rescued by the Fine Prince.
The Happiness-Ever-After.
That was worth anything.
It was good to be a "maid mild."
That made the breath go fast.

Her bacon burned. She
Hastened to hide it in the step-on can, and
Drew more strips from the meat case. The eggs and sour-
milk biscuits

Did well. She set out a jar
Of her new quince preserve.

. . . But there was a something about the matter of the Dark Villain.
He should have been older, perhaps.
The hacking down of a villain was more fun to think about
When his menace possessed undisputed breadth, undisputed height,
And a harsh kind of vice.
And best of all, when his history was cluttered
With the bones of many eaten knights and princesses.

The fun was disturbed, then all but nullified
When the Dark Villain was a blackish child
Of fourteen, with eyes still too young to be dirty,
And a mouth too young to have lost every reminder
Of its infant softness.

That boy must have been surprised! For
These were grown-ups. Grown-ups were supposed to be wise.
And the Fine Prince — and that other — so tall, so broad, so
Grown! Perhaps the boy had never guessed
That the trouble with grown-ups was that under the magnificent shell of adulthood, just under,
Waited the baby full of tantrums.

It occurred to her that there may have been something
Ridiculous in the picture of the Fine Prince
Rushing (rich with the breadth and height and
Mature solidness whose lack, in the Dark Villain, was impressing her,
Confronting her more and more as this first day after the trial
And acquittal wore on) rushing
With his heavy companion to hack down (unhorsed)
That little foe.
So much had happened, she could not remember now what that foe had done
Against her, or if anything had been done.
The one thing in the world that she did know and knew
With terrifying clarity was that her composition
Had disintegrated. That, although the pattern prevailed,
The breaks were everywhere. That she could think
Of no thread capable of the necessary
Sew-work.

She made the babies sit in their places at the table.
Then, before calling Him, she hurried
To the mirror with her comb and lipstick. It was necessary
To be more beautiful than ever.
The beautiful wife.
For sometimes she fancied he looked at her as though
Measuring her. As if he considered, Had she been worth It?

Had *she* been worth the blood, the cramped cries, the little stuttering bravado,
The gradual dulling of those Negro eyes,
The sudden, overwhelming *little-boyness* in that barn?
Whatever she might feel or half-feel, the lipstick necessity was something apart. He must never conclude
That she had not been worth It.

He sat down, the Fine Prince, and
Began buttering a biscuit. He looked at his hands.
He twisted in his chair, he scratched his nose.
He glanced again, almost secretly, at his hands.
More papers were in from the North, he mumbled. More meddling headlines.
With their pepper-words, "bestiality," and "barbarism," and
"Shocking."
The half-sneers he had mastered for the trial worked across
His sweet and pretty face.

What he'd like to do, he explained, was kill them all.
The time lost. The unwanted fame.
Still, it had been fun to show those intruders
A thing or two. To show that snappy-eyed mother,
That sassy, Northern, brown-black ——

Nothing could stop Mississippi.

He knew that. Big Fella
Knew that.
And, what was so good, Mississippi knew that.
Nothing and nothing could stop Mississippi.
They could send in their petitions, and scar
Their newspapers with bleeding headlines. Their governors
Could appeal to Washington. . . .

"What I want," the older baby said, "is 'lasses on my jam."
Whereupon the younger baby
Picked up the molasses pitcher and threw
The molasses in his brother's face. Instantly
The Fine Prince leaned across the table and slapped
The small and smiling criminal.

She did not speak. When the Hand
Came down and away, and she could look at her child,
At her baby-child,
She could think only of blood.
Surely her baby's cheek
Had disappeared, and in its place, surely,
Hung a heaviness, a lengthening red, a red that had no end.
She shook her head. It was not true, of course.
It was not true at all. The
Child's face was as always, the
Color of the paste in her paste-jar.

She left the table, to the tune of the children's lamentations, which were shriller
Than ever. She
Looked out of a window. She said not a word. *That*
Was one of the new Somethings —
The fear,
Tying her as with iron.

Suddenly she felt his hands upon her. He had followed her
To the window. The children were whimpering now.
Such bits of tots. And she, their mother,
Could not protect them. She looked at her shoulders, still
Gripped in the claim of his hands. She tried, but could not resist the idea
That a red ooze was seeping, spreading darkly, thickly, slowly,
Over her white shoulders, her own shoulders,
And over all of Earth and Mars.

He whispered something to her, did the Fine Prince, something
About love, something about love and night and intention.

She heard no hoof-beat of the horse and saw no flash of the shining steel.

He pulled her face around to meet
His, and there it was, close close,

For the first time in all those days and nights.
His mouth, wet and red,
So very, very, very red,
Closed over hers.

Then a sickness heaved within her. The courtroom Coca-
Cola,
The courtroom beer and hate and sweat and drone,
Pushed like a wall against her. She wanted to bear it.
But his mouth would not go away and neither would the
Decapitated exclamation points in that Other Woman's
eyes.

She did not scream.
She stood there.
But a hatred for him burst into glorious flower,
And its perfume enclasped them—big,
Bigger than all magnolias.

The last bleak news of the ballad.
The rest of the rugged music.
The last quatrain.

The Last Quatrain of the Ballad of Emmett Till

AFTER THE MURDER,
AFTER THE BURIAL

Emmett's mother is a pretty-faced thing;
the tint of pulled taffy.
She sits in a red room,
drinking black coffee.
She kisses her killed boy.
And she is sorry.
Chaos in windy grays
through a red prairie.

Mrs. Small

Mrs. Small went to the kitchen for her pocketbook
And came back to the living room with a peculiar look
And the coffee pot.
Pocketbook. Pot.
Pot. Pocketbook.

The insurance man was waiting there
With superb and cared-for hair.
His face did not have much time.
He did not glance with sublime
Love upon the little plump tan woman
With the half-open mouth and the half-mad eyes
And the smile half-human
Who stood in the middle of the living-room floor planning
apple pies
And graciously offering him a steaming coffee pot.
Pocketbook. Pot.

"Oh!" Mrs. Small came to her senses,
Peered earnestly through thick lenses,

Jumped terribly. This, too, was a mistake,
Unforgivable no matter how much she had to bake.
For there can be no whiter whiteness than this one:
An insurance man's shirt on its morning run.
This Mrs. Small now soiled
With a pair of brown
Spurts (just recently boiled)
Of the "very best coffee in town."

"The best coffee in town is what *you* make, Delphine! There
is none dandier!"
Those were the words of the pleased Jim Small —
Who was no bandier of words at all.
Jim Small was likely to give you a good swat
When he was *not*
Pleased. He was, absolutely, no bandier.

"I don't know where my mind is this morning,"
Said Mrs. Small, scorning
Apologies! For there was so much
For which to apologize! Oh such
Mountains of things, she'd never get anything done
If she begged forgiveness for each one.

She paid him.

But apologies and her hurry would not mix.
The six

Daughters were a-yell, a-scramble, in the hall. The four
Sons (horrors) could not be heard any more.

No.
The insurance man would have to glare
Idiotically into her own sterile stare
A moment — then depart,
Leaving her to release her heart
And dizziness
And silence her six
And mix
Her spices and core
And slice her apples, and find her four.
Continuing her part
Of the world's business.

Jessie Mitchell's Mother

Into her mother's bedroom to wash the ballooning body.
"My mother is jelly-hearted and she has a brain of jelly:
Sweet, quiver-soft, irrelevant. Not essential.
Only a habit would cry if she should die.
A pleasant sort of fool without the least iron. . . .
Are you better, mother, do you think it will come today?"
The stretched yellow rag that was Jessie Mitchell's mother
Reviewed her. Young, and so thin, and so straight.
So straight! as if nothing could ever bend her.
But poor men would bend her, and doing things with poor
men,
Being much in bed, and babies would bend her over,
And the rest of things in life that were for poor women,
Coming to them grinning and pretty with intent to bend
and to kill.
Comparisons shattered her heart, ate at her bulwarks:
The shabby and the bright: she, almost hating her
daughter,
Crept into an old sly refuge: "Jessie's black
And her way will be black, and jerkier even than mine.

Mine, in fact, because I was lovely, had flowers
Tucked in the jerks, flowers were here and there. . . ."
She revived for the moment settled and dried-up triumphs,
Forced perfume into old petals, pulled up the droop,
Refueled
Triumphant long-exhaled breaths.
Her exquisite yellow youth. . . .

The Chicago Defender *Sends a Man to Little Rock*

FALL, 1957

In Little Rock the people bear
Babes, and comb and part their hair
And watch the want ads, put repair
To roof and latch. While wheat toast burns
A woman waters multiferns.

Time upholds or overturns
The many, tight, and small concerns.

In Little Rock the people sing
Sunday hymns like anything,
Through Sunday pomp and polishing.

And after testament and tunes,
Some soften Sunday afternoons
With lemon tea and Lorna Doones.

I forecast

And I believe
Come Christmas Little Rock will cleave
To Christmas tree and trifle, weave,
From laugh and tinsel, texture fast.

In Little Rock is baseball; Barcarolle.
That hotness in July . . . the uniformed figures raw and
  implacable
And not intellectual,
Batting the hotness or clawing the suffering dust.
The Open Air Concert, on the special twilight green . . .
When Beethoven is brutal or whispers to lady-like air.
Blanket-sitters are solemn, as Johann troubles to lean
To tell them what to mean. . . .

There is love, too, in Little Rock. Soft women softly
Opening themselves in kindness,
Or, pitying one's blindness,
Awaiting one's pleasure
In azure
Glory with anguished rose at the root. . . .
To wash away old semi-discomfitures.
They re-teach purple and unsullen blue.
The wispy soils go. And uncertain
Half-havings have they clarified to sures.

In Little Rock they know
Not answering the telephone is a way of rejecting life,

That it is our business to be bothered, is our business
To cherish bores or boredom, be polite
To lies and love and many-faceted fuzziness.

I scratch my head, massage the hate-I-had.
I blink across my prim and pencilled pad.
The saga I was sent for is not down.
Because there is a puzzle in this town.
The biggest News I do not dare
Telegraph to the Editor's chair:
"They are like people everywhere."

The angry Editor would reply
In hundred harryings of Why.

And true, they are hurling spittle, rock,
Garbage and fruit in Little Rock.
And I saw coiling storm a-writhe
On bright madonnas. And a scythe
Of men harassing brownish girls.
(The bows and barrettes in the curls
And braids declined away from joy.)

I saw a bleeding brownish boy. . . .

The lariat lynch-wish I deplored.

The loveliest lynchee was our Lord.

The Lovers of the Poor

arrive. The Ladies from the Ladies' Betterment
League
Arrive in the afternoon, the late light slanting
In diluted gold bars across the boulevard brag
Of proud, seamed faces with mercy and murder hinting
Here, there, interrupting, all deep and debonair,
The pink paint on the innocence of fear;
Walk in a gingerly manner up the hall.
Cutting with knives served by their softest care,
Served by their love, so barbarously fair.
Whose mothers taught: You'd better not be cruel!
You had better not throw stones upon the wrens!
Herein they kiss and coddle and assault
Anew and dearly in the innocence
With which they baffle nature. Who are full,
Sleek, tender-clad, fit, fiftyish, a-glow, all
Sweetly abortive, hinting at fat fruit,
Judge it high time that fiftyish fingers felt
Beneath the lovelier planes of enterprise.
To resurrect. To moisten with milky chill.

To be a random hitching post or plush.
To be, for wet eyes, random and handy hem.

Their guild is giving money to the poor.
The worthy poor. The very very worthy
And beautiful poor. Perhaps just not too swarthy?
Perhaps just not too dirty nor too dim
Nor — passionate. In truth, what they could wish
Is — something less than derelict or dull.
Not staunch enough to stab, though, gaze for gaze!
God shield them sharply from the beggar-bold!
The noxious needy ones whose battle's bald
Nonetheless for being voiceless, hits one down.

But it's all so bad! and entirely too much for them.
The stench; the urine, cabbage, and dead beans,
Dead porridges of assorted dusty grains,
The old smoke, *heavy* diapers, and, they're told,
Something called chitterlings. The darkness. Drawn
Darkness, or dirty light. The soil that stirs.
The soil that looks the soil of centuries.
And for that matter the *general* oldness. Old
Wood. Old marble. Old tile. Old old old.
Not homekind Oldness! Not Lake Forest, Glencoe.
Nothing is sturdy, nothing is majestic,
There is no quiet drama, no rubbed glaze, no
Unkillable infirmity of such
A tasteful turn as lately they have left,
Glencoe, Lake Forest, and to which their cars
Must presently restore them. When they're done

With dullards and distortions of this fistic
Patience of the poor and put-upon.
        They've never seen such a make-do-ness as
Newspaper rugs before! In this, this "flat,"
Their hostess is gathering up the oozed, the rich
Rugs of the morning (tattered! the bespattered . . .),
Readies to spread clean rugs for afternoon.
Here is a scene for you. The Ladies look,
In horror, behind a substantial citizeness
Whose trains clank out across her swollen heart.
Who, arms akimbo, almost fills a door.
All tumbling children, quilts dragged to the floor
And tortured thereover, potato peelings, soft-
Eyed kitten, hunched-up, haggard, to-be-hurt.
        Their League is allotting largesse to the Lost.
But to put their clean, their pretty money, to put
Their money collected from delicate rose-fingers
Tipped with their hundred flawless rose-nails seems . . .
        They own Spode, Lowestoft, candelabra,
Mantels, and hostess gowns, and sunburst clocks,
Turtle soup, Chippendale, red satin "hangings,"
Aubussons and Hattie Carnegie. They Winter
In Palm Beach; cross the Water in June; attend,
When suitable, the nice Art Institute;
Buy the right books in the best bindings; saunter
On Michigan, Easter mornings, in sun or wind.
Oh Squalor! This sick four-story hulk, this fibre
With fissures everywhere! Why, what are bringings

Of loathe-love largesse? What shall peril hungers
So old old, what shall flatter the desolate?
Tin can, blocked fire escape and chitterling
And swaggering seeking youth and the puzzled wreckage
Of the middle passage, and urine and stale shames
And, again, the porridges of the underslung
And children children children. Heavens! That
Was a rat, surely, off there, in the shadows? Long
And long-tailed? Gray? The Ladies from the Ladies'
Betterment League agree it will be better
To achieve the outer air that rights and steadies,
To hie to a house that does not holler, to ring
Bells elsetime, better presently to cater
To no more Possibilities, to get
Away. Perhaps the money can be posted.
Perhaps they two may choose another Slum!
Some serious sooty half-unhappy home!—
Where loathe-love likelier may be invested.

Keeping their scented bodies in the center
Of the hall as they walk down the hysterical hall,
They allow their lovely skirts to graze no wall,
Are off at what they manage of a canter,
And, resuming all the clues of what they were,
Try to avoid inhaling the laden air.

A Sunset of the City

KATHLEEN EILEEN

Already I am no longer looked at with lechery or love.
My daughters and sons have put me away with marbles and dolls,
Are gone from the house.
My husband and lovers are pleasant or somewhat polite
And night is night.

It is a real chill out,
The genuine thing.
I am not deceived, I do not think it is still summer
Because sun stays and birds continue to sing.

It is summer-gone that I see, it is summer-gone.
The sweet flowers indrying and dying down,
The grasses forgetting their blaze and consenting to brown.

It is a real chill out. The fall crisp comes.

I am aware there is winter to heed.
There is no warm house
That is fitted with my need.

I am cold in this cold house this house
Whose washed echoes are tremulous down lost halls.
I am a woman, and dusty, standing among new affairs.
I am a woman who hurries through her prayers.

Tin intimations of a quiet core to be my
Desert and my dear relief
Come: there shall be such islanding from grief,
And small communion with the master shore.
Twang they. And I incline this ear to tin,
Consult a dual dilemma. Whether to dry
In humming pallor or to leap and die.

Somebody muffed it? Somebody wanted to joke.

A Man of the Middle Class

I'm what has gone out blithely and with noise
Returning! I'm what rushed around to pare
Down rind, to find fruit frozen under there.

I am bedraggled, with sundry dusts to be shed;
Trailing desperate tarnished tassels. These strident Aprils
With terrifying polkas and Bugle Calls
Confound me.

— Although I've risen! and my back is bold.
My tongue is brainy, choosing from among
Care, rage, surprise, despair, and choosing care.
I'm semi-splendid within what I've defended.

Yet, there I totter, there limp laxly. My
Uncomely trudge
To Plateau That and platitudinous Plateau
Whichever is no darling to my grudge-
Choked industry or usual alcohol.

I've roses to guard
In the architectural prettiness of my yard.
(But there are no paths remarkable for wide
Believable welcomes.)

I have loved directions.
I have loved orders and an iron to stride, I,
Whose hands are papers now,
Fit only for tossing in this outrageous air.

Not God nor grace nor candy balls
Will get me everything different and the same!

My wife has canvas walls.

My wife never quite forgets to put flowers in vases,
Bizarre prints in the most unusual places,
Give teas for poets, wear odoriferous furs.
An awful blooming is hers.

I've antique firearms. Blackamoors. Chinese
Rugs. Ivories.
Bronzes. Everything I Wanted.
But have I answers? Oh methinks
I've answers such as have
The executives I copied long ago,
The ones who, forfeiting Vicks salve,
Prayer book and Mother, shot themselves last Sunday.

All forsaking
All that was theirs but for their money's taking.
I've answers such as Giants used to know.
There's a Giant who'll jump next Monday; all forsaking
Wives, safes and solitaire
And the elegant statue standing at the foot of the stair.

Kid Bruin

ARRANGES ANOTHER TITLE DEFENSE

I rode into the golden yell
Of the hollow land of fame.
And when I mentioned rainbow
They did not know the name;

But thought it might have been there
And overnight have hied:
Adding that nothing in that land
Could be trapped or tied.
Trapped or tied or kissed for good
Or bound about the hand.

They could not swear to rainbow
In that hollow land.

The Ghost at the Quincy Club

All filmy down she drifts
In filmy stuffs and all.
Some gentle Gentile girl
Wafts down our Quincy hall.
This was a mansion once! —
With polished panels and all.

Where velvet voices lessened, stopped, and rose
Rise raucous Howdys. And a curse comes pure.
Yea it comes pure and challenges again
All ghost airs, graces, all daughters-of-gentlemen
Moth-soft, off-sweet. Demure.

Where Tea and Father were (each clear
And lemony) are dark folk, drinking beer.

The Crazy Woman

I shall not sing a May song.
A May song should be gay.
I'll wait until November
And sing a song of gray.

I'll wait until November.
That is the time for me.
I'll go out in the frosty dark
And sing most terribly.

And all the little people
Will stare at me and say,
"That is the Crazy Woman
Who would not sing in May."

Pete at the Zoo

I wonder if the elephant
Is lonely in his stall
When all the boys and girls are gone
And there's no shout at all,
And there's no one to stamp before,
No one to note his might.
Does he hunch up, as I do,
Against the dark of night?

Bronzeville Man with a Belt in the Back

In such an armor he may rise and raid
The dark cave after midnight, unafraid,
And slice the shadows with his able sword
Of good broad nonchalance, hashing them down.

And come out and accept the gasping crowd,
Shake off the praises with an airiness.
And, searching, see love shining in an eye,
But never smile.

In such an armor he cannot be slain.

A Lovely Love

LILLIAN'S

Let it be alleys. Let it be a hall
Whose janitor javelins epithet and thought
To cheapen hyacinth darkness that we sought
And played we found, rot, make the petals fall.
Let it be stairways, and a splintery box
Where you have thrown me, scraped me with your kiss,
Have honed me, have released me after this
Cavern kindness, smiled away our shocks.
That is the birthright of our lovely love
In swaddling clothes. Not like that Other one.
Not lit by any fondling star above.
Not found by any wise men, either. Run.
People are coming. They must not catch us here
Definitionless in this strict atmosphere.

For Clarice It Is Terrible Because with This He Takes Away All the Popular Songs and the Moonlights and Still Night Hushes and the Movies with Star-eyed Girls and Simpering Males

They were going to have so much fun in the summer.
But winter has come to the edges of his regard.
Not the lace-ice, but the bleak, the bleak steep sorrow.
Not the shy snow, not the impermanent icicles but the hard
The cruel pack and snarl of the unloved cold.

There is nowhere for her to go.
There is no tenderness on whom she may frankly cry.
There is no way to unlatch her face
And show the gray shudder
Of this hurt hour
And the desert death of tomorrow.

Jack

is not spendthrift of faith.
He has a skinny eye.
He spends a wariness of faith.
He puts his other by.

And comes it up his faith bought true,
He spends a little more.
And comes it up his faith bought false,
It's long gone from the store.

A Penitent Considers Another Coming of Mary

FOR REVEREND THEODORE RICHARDSON

If Mary came would Mary
Forgive, as Mothers may,
And sad and second Saviour
Furnish us today?

She would not shake her head and leave
This military air,
But ratify a modern hay,
And put her Baby there.

Mary would not punish men —
If Mary came again.

Bronzeville Woman in a Red Hat

HIRES OUT TO
MRS. MILES

I

They had never had one in the house before.
        The strangeness of it all. Like unleashing
A lion, really. Poised
To pounce. A puma. A panther. A black
Bear.
There it stood in the door,
Under a red hat that was rash, but refreshing —
In a tasteless way, of course — across the dull dare,
The semi-assault of that extraordinary blackness.
The slackness
Of that light pink mouth told little. The eyes told of heavy
  care. . . .
But that was neither here nor there,
And nothing to a wage-paying mistress as should
Be getting her due whether life had been good
For her slave, or bad.

There it stood
In the door. They had never had
One in the house before.

But the Irishwoman had left!
A message had come.
Something about a murder at home.
A daughter's husband — "berserk," that was the phrase:
The dear man had "gone berserk"
And short work —
With a hammer — had been made
Of this daughter and her nights and days.
The Irishwoman (underpaid,
Mrs. Miles remembered with smiles),
Who was a perfect jewel, a red-faced trump,
A good old sort, a baker
Of rum cake, a maker
Of Mustard, would never return.
Mrs. Miles had begged the bewitched woman
To finish, at least, the biscuit blending,
To tarry till the curry was done,
To show some concern
For the burning soup, to attend to the tending
Of the tossed salad. "Inhuman,"
Patsy Houlihan had called Mrs. Miles.
"Inhuman." And "a fool."
And "a cool
One."

The Alert Agency had leafed through its files —
On short notice could offer
Only this dusky duffer
That now made its way to her kitchen and sat on her
kitchen stool.

II

Her creamy child kissed by the black maid! square on the
mouth!
World yelled, world writhed, world turned to light and
rolled
Into her kitchen, nearly knocked her down.

Quotations, of course, from baby books were great
Ready armor; (but her animal distress
Wore, too and under, a subtler metal dress,
Inheritance of approximately hate).
Say baby shrieked to see his finger bleed,
Wished human humoring — there was a kind
Of unintimate love, a love more of the mind
To order the nebulousness of that need.
— This was the way to put it, this the relief.
This sprayed a honey upon marvelous grime.
This told it possible to postpone the reef.
Fashioned a huggable darling out of crime.
Made monster personable in personal sight
By cracking mirrors down the personal night.

Disgust crawled through her as she chased the theme.
She, quite supposing purity despoiled,
Committed to sourness, disordered, soiled,
Went in to pry the ordure from the cream.
Cooing, "Come." (Come out of the cannibal wilderness,
Dirt, dark, into the sun and bloomful air.
Return to freshness of your right world, wear
Sweetness again. Be done with beast, duress.)

Child with continuing cling issued his No in final fire,
Kissed back the colored maid,
Not wise enough to freeze or be afraid.
Conscious of kindness, easy creature bond.
Love had been handy and rapid to respond.

Heat at the hairline, heat between the bowels,
Examining seeming coarse unnatural scene,
She saw all things except herself serene:
Child, big black woman, pretty kitchen towels.

The Contemplation of Suicide: The Temptation of Timothy

One poises, poses, at track, or range, or river,
Saying, What is the fact of my life, to what do I tend? —
And is it assured and sweet that I have come, after mazes and robins, after the foodless swallowings and snatchings at fog, to this foppish end?
(Knowing that downtown the sluggish shrug their shoulders, slink, talk.)

Then, though one can think of no fact, no path, no ground,
Some little thing, remarkless and daily, relates
Its common cliché. One lunges or lags on, prates. —
Too selfish to be nothing while beams break, surf's epileptic, chicken reeks or squalls.

On the Occasion of the Open-air Formation of the Olde Tymers' Walking and Nature Club

We shall go playing in the woods again!
The flowers and fruits and nuts and sun have waited.
And when we come, we merry girls and men,
They will unlock themselves, and be elated.

And we shall walk among them, working well
At this delicious business of being gay.
And we shall push our laughter like a bell,
Trying to make it ring in the old way.

But if our romp is rusty, if we fumble,
If we fall down, and if our festival
Of molded mirth should crack, or even crumble,
Have mercy, flowers! sun, forgive us all.

Bessie of Bronzeville Visits Mary and Norman at a Beach-house in New Buffalo

You said, "Now take your shoes off," while what played
Was not the back-town boogie but a green
Wet music stuff, above the wide and clean
Sand, and my hand laughed.
Toes urged the slab to amber foam.

And I was hurt by cider in the air.
And what the lake-wash did was dizzying.
I thought of England, as I watched you bring
The speckled pebbles,
The smooth quartz; I thought of Italy.

Italy and England come.
A sea sits up and starts to sing to me.

Naomi

Too foraging to blue-print or deploy! —
To lift her brother;
Or tell dull mother
That is not it among the dishes and brooms,
It is damper
Than what you will wipe out of sills and down from the mouldings of rooms
And dump from the dirty-clothes hamper;

Or say "Do not bother
To hug your cheese and furniture"
To her small father;

Or to register at all the hope of her hunt or say what
It was not.

(It was, by diligent caring,
To find out what life was for.

For certainly what it was not for was forbearing.)

Callie Ford

It's a day for running out of town
With a man whose eyes are brown.

We'll go where trees leap up out of hills
And flowers are not planned.
We'll be happy all our day.
First, he must press my hand,
In the afternoon discover my waist,
At night my mouth, and ask for the taste.
And he must call me "very sweet."
And I must call him "clever."

We'll come back
Together at dawn
And hate each other forever.

The Ballad of Rudolph Reed

Rudolph Reed was oaken.
His wife was oaken too.
And his two good girls and his good little man
Oakened as they grew.

"I am not hungry for berries.
I am not hungry for bread.
But hungry hungry for a house
Where at night a man in bed

"May never hear the plaster
Stir as if in pain.
May never hear the roaches
Falling like fat rain.

"Where never wife and children need
Go blinking through the gloom.
Where every room of many rooms
Will be full of room.

"Oh my home may have its east or west
Or north or south behind it.
All I know is I shall know it,
And fight for it when I find it."

It was in a street of bitter white
That he made his application.
For Rudolph Reed was oakener
Than others in the nation.

The agent's steep and steady stare
Corroded to a grin.
Why, you black old, tough old hell of a man,
Move your family in!

Nary a grin grinned Rudolph Reed,
Nary a curse cursed he,
But moved in his House. With his dark little wife,
And his dark little children three.

A neighbor would *look*, with a yawning eye
That squeezed into a slit.
But the Rudolph Reeds and the children three
Were too joyous to notice it.

For were they not firm in a home of their own
With windows everywhere
And a beautiful banistered stair
And a front yard for flowers and a back yard for grass?

The first night, a rock, big as two fists.
The second, a rock big as three.
But nary a curse cursed Rudolph Reed.
(Though oaken as man could be.)

The third night, a silvery ring of glass.
Patience ached to endure.
But he looked, and lo! small Mabel's blood
Was staining her gaze so pure.

Then up did rise our Rudolph Reed
And pressed the hand of his wife,
And went to the door with a thirty-four
And a beastly butcher knife.

He ran like a mad thing into the night.
And the words in his mouth were stinking.
By the time he had hurt his first white man
He was no longer thinking.

By the time he had hurt his fourth white man
Rudolph Reed was dead.
His neighbors gathered and kicked his corpse.
"Nigger —" his neighbors said.

Small Mabel whimpered all night long,
For calling herself the cause.
Her oak-eyed mother did no thing
But change the bloody gauze.

Priscilla Assails the Sepulchre of Love

I can't unlock my eyes because
My body will come through
And cut her every clothing off
And drive herself to you

Who want no sort of gift outright
Nor one that simpers back
Nor one that sorrows off, but none,
And laugh above your lack.

I keep my keys away that she
May never have to find
The enameled winter of your heart,
The pastels of your mind.

Leftist Orator in Washington Park Pleasantly Punishes the Gropers

Poor Pale-eyed, thrice-gulping Amazed.
It is white and rushed here, this is a crazy snow.
I am afraid the wind will not falter at any time in the night.
I know you are frightened and I know
You know not where to go.

I foretell the heat and yawn of eye and the drop of the mouth and the screech,
The foolish, unhappy screech hanging high on the air.
Because you had no dream or belief or reach.
Because you could only beseech.

Because you were nothing, saw nothing, did nothing at all.
Because there will be No Thing for which you fall.

The Artists' and Models' Ball

(FOR FRANK SHEPHERD)

Wonders do not confuse. We call them that
And close the matter there. But common things
Surprise us. They accept the names we give
With calm, and keep them. Easy-breathing then
We brave our next small business. Well, behind
Our backs they alter. How were we to know.

The Egg Boiler

Being you, you cut your poetry from wood.
The boiling of an egg is heavy art.
You come upon it as an artist should,
With rich-eyed passion, and with straining heart.
We fools, we cut our poems out of air,
Night color, wind soprano, and such stuff.
And sometimes weightlessness is much to bear.
You mock it, though, you name it Not Enough.
The egg, spooned gently to the avid pan,
And left the strict three minutes, or the four,
Is your Enough and art for any man.
We fools give courteous ear — then cut some more,
Shaping a gorgeous Nothingness from cloud.
You watch us, eat your egg, and laugh aloud.

In Emanuel's Nightmare:
Another Coming of Christ

(SPEAKS, AMONG SPIRIT QUESTIONERS, OF MARVELOUS SPIRIT AFFAIRS)

There had been quiet all that afternoon.
Just such a quiet afternoon as any,
Though with a brighter and a freer air.
The sleepy sun sat on us, and those clouds
Dragged dreamily. Well, it was interesting —
How silence could give place to such a noise.
But now — is noise the word? Is that exact?
I think not.

I'll try to name it. Naming is my line.
I won the Great War-Naming Contest. Ah,
I put it over on them all. I beat
Them all. I wear an honor on my name —

Sound wasn't in it. Though it was loud enough.
I'd say it was a heat.

But it took us. Did with us as it would.
Wound us in balls, unraveled, wound again.
And women screamed "The Judgment Day has come."
And little children gathered up the cry.
It was then that they knocked each other down
To get to — Where? But they were used to Doors.
Thought they had but to beat their Fellow Man
To get to and get out of one again.

It wasn't Judgment Day. (For we are here.)
And presently the people knew, and sighed.
Out of that heaven a most beautiful Man
Came down. But now is coming quite the word?
It wasn't coming. I'd say it was — a Birth.
The man was born out of the heaven, in truth.
Yet no parturient creature ever knew
That naturalness, that hurtlessness, that ease.

How He was tall and strong!
How He was cold-browed! How He mildly smiled!
How the voice played on the heavy hope of the air
And loved our hearts out!
Why, it was such a voice as gave me eyes
To see my Fellow Man of all the world,
There with me, listening.

He had come down, He said, to clean the earth
Of the dirtiness of war.

Now tell of why His power failed Him there?
His power did not fail. It was that, simply,
He found how much the people wanted war.
How much it was their creed, and their good joy.
And what they lived for. He had not the heart
To take away their chief sweet delectation.

We tear — as a decent gesture, a tact — we tear
Laxly again at our lax, our tired hair.

The people wanted war. War's in their hearts.
    (In me, in your snag-toothed fool
Who won the Great War-Naming Contest and
All the years since has bragged how he did Beat
His Fellow Man.) It is the human aim.
Without, there would be no hate. No Diplomats.
And households would be fresh and frictionless.

God's Son went home. Among us it is whispered
He cried the tears of men.

Feeling, in fact,
We have no need of peace.

1963

RIDERS TO THE BLOOD-RED WRATH

My proper prudence toward his proper probe
Astonished their ancestral seemliness.
It was a not-nice risk, a wrought risk, was
An indelicate risk, they thought. And an excess.
Howas I handled my discordances
And prides and apoplectic ice, howas
I reined my charger, channeled the fit fume
Of his most splendid honorable jazz
Escaped the closing and averted sight
Waiving all witness except of rotted flowers
Framed in maimed velvet. That mad demi-art
Of ancient and irrevocable hours.
Waiving all witness except of dimnesses
From which extrude beloved and pennant arms
Of a renegade death impatient at his shrine
And keen to share the gases of his charms.
They veer to vintage. Careening from tomorrows.
Blaring away from my just genesis.
They loot Last Night. They hug old graves, root up
Decomposition, warm it with a kiss.

The National Anthem vampires at the blood.
I am a uniform. Not brusque. I bray

Through blur and blunder in a little voice!
This is a tender grandeur, a tied fray!
Under macabres, stratagem and fair
Fine smiles upon the face of holocaust,
My scream! unedited, unfrivolous.
My laboring unlatched braid of heat and frost.
I hurt. I keep that scream in at what pain:
At what repeal of salvage and eclipse.
Army unhonored, meriting the gold, I
Have sewn my guns inside my burning lips.

Did they detect my parleys and replies?
My Revolution pushed his twin the mare,
The she-thing with the soft eyes that conspire
To lull off men, before him everywhere.
Perhaps they could not see what wheedling bent
Her various heart in mottles of submission
And sent her into a firm skirmish which
Has tickled out the enemy's sedition.

They do not see how deftly I endure.
Deep down the whirlwind of good rage I store
Commemorations in an utter thrall.
Although I need not eat them any more.

I remember kings.
A blossoming palace. Silver. Ivory.
The conventional wealth of stalking Africa.
All bright, all Bestial. Snarling marvelously.

I remember my right to roughly run and roar.
My right to raid the sun, consult the moon,
Nod to my princesses or split them open,
To flay my lions, eat blood with a spoon.
You never saw such running and such roaring!—
Nor heard a burgeoning heart so craze and pound!—
Nor sprang to such a happy rape of heaven!
Nor sanctioned such a kinship with the ground!

And I remember blazing dementias
Aboard such trade as maddens any man.
. . . The mate and captain fragrantly reviewed
The fragrant hold and presently began
Their retching rampage among their luminous
Black pudding, among the guttural chained slime:
Half fainting from their love affair with fetors
That pledged a haughty allegiance for all time.

I recollect the latter lease and lash
And labor that defiled the bone, that thinned
My blood and blood-line. All my climate my
Foster designers designed and disciplined.

But my detention and my massive stain,
And my distortion and my Calvary
I grind into a little light lorgnette
Most sly: to read man's inhumanity.
And I remark my Matter is not all.

Man's chopped in China, in India indented.
From Israel what's Arab is resented.
Europe candies custody and war.

Behind my exposé
I formalize my pity: "J shall cite,
Star, and esteem all that which is of woman,
Human and hardly human."

Democracy and Christianity
Recommence with me.

And I ride ride I ride on to the end—
Where glowers my continuing Calvary.
I,
My fellows, and those canny consorts of
Our spread hands in this contretemps-for-love
Ride into wrath, wraith and menagerie

To fail, to flourish, to wither or to win.
We lurch, distribute, we extend, begin.

THE EMPTY WOMAN

The empty woman took toys!
          In her sisters' homes
Were little girls and boys.

The empty woman had hats
To show. With feathers. Wore combs
In polished waves. Wooed cats

And pigeons. Shopped.
Shopped hard for nephew-toys,
Niece-toys. Made taffy. Popped

Popcorn and hated her sisters,
Featherless and waveless but able to
Mend measles, nag noses, blast blisters

And all day waste wordful girls
And war-boys, and all day
Say "Oh God!"—and tire among curls

And plump legs and proud muscle
And blackened school-bags, babushkas, torn socks,
And bouffants that bustle, and rustle.

TO BE IN LOVE

To be in love
Is to touch things with a lighter hand.

In yourself you stretch, you are well.

You look at things
Through his eyes.
A Cardinal is red.
A sky is blue.
Suddenly you know he knows too.
He is not there but
You know you are tasting together
The winter, or light spring weather.

His hand to take your hand is overmuch.
Too much to bear.

You cannot look in his eyes
Because your pulse must not say
What must not be said.

When he
Shuts a door—

Is not there—
Your arms are water.

And you are free
With a ghastly freedom.

You are the beautiful half
Of a golden hurt.

You remember and covet his mouth,
To touch, to whisper on.

Oh when to declare
Is certain Death!

Oh when to apprize
Is to mesmerize,

To see fall down, the Column of Gold,
Into the commonest ash.

is merry glory.
Is saltatory.
Yet grips his right of twisting free.

Has a long reach,
Strong speech,
Remedial fears.
Muscular tears.

Holds horticulture
In the eye of the vulture
Infirm profession.
In the Compression—
In mud and blood and sudden death—
In the breath
Of the holocaust he
Is helmsman, hatchet, headlight.
See
One restless in the exotic time! and ever,
Till the air is cured of its fever.

A CATCH OF SHY FISH

garbageman: the man with the orderly mind

What do you think of us in fuzzy endeavor, you whose directions are sterling, whose lunge is straight?
Can you make a reason, how can you pardon us who memorize the rules and never score?
Who memorize the rules from your own text but never quite transfer them to the game,
Who never quite receive the whistling ball, who gawk, begin to absorb the crowd's own roar.

Is earnestness enough, may earnestness attract or lead to light;
Is light enough, if hands in clumsy frenzy, flimsy whimsicality, enlist;
Is light enough when this bewilderment crying against the dark shuts down the shades?
Dilute confusion. Find and explode our mist.

sick man looks at flowers

You are sick and old, and there is a closing in—
The eyes gone dead to all that would beguile.

Echoes are dull and the body accepts no touch
Except its pain. Mind is a little isle.

But now invades this impudence of red!
This ripe rebuke, this burgeoning affluence
Mocks me and mocks the desert of my bed.

old people working (garden, car)

Old people working. Making a gift of garden.
Or washing a car, so some one else may ride.
A note of alliance, an eloquence of pride.
A way of greeting or sally to the world.

weaponed woman

Well, life has been a baffled vehicle
And baffling. But she fights, and
Has fought, according to her lights and
The lenience of her whirling-place.

She fights with semi-folded arms,
Her strong bag, and the stiff
Frost of her face (that challenges "When" and "If.")
And altogether she does Rather Well.

old tennis player

Refuses
To refuse the racket, to mutter No to the net.
He leans to life, conspires to give and get
Other serving yet.

a surrealist and Omega

Omega ran to witness him; beseeched;
Brought caution and carnality and cash.
She sauced him brownly, eating him
Under her fancy's finest Worcestershire.

He zigzagged.
He was a knotted hiss.
He was an insane hash
Of rebellious small strengths
And soft-mouthed mumbling weakness.

The art
Would not come right. That smear,
That yellow in the gray corner—
That was not right, he had not reached
The right, the careless flailed-out bleakness.

A god, a child.
He said he was most seriously amiss.

She had no purple or pearl to hang
About the neck of one a-wild.

A bantam beauty
Loving his ownhood for all it was worth.

Spaulding and Francois

There are cloudlets and things of cool silver in our dream,
there are all of the Things Ethereal.

There is a
Scent of wind cut with pine, a noise of
Wind tangled among bells. There is spiritual laughter
Too hushed to be gay, too high: the happiness
Of angels. And there are angels' eyes, soft,
Heavy with precious compulsion.

But the People
Will not let us alone; will not credit, condone
Art-loves that shun
Them (moderate Christians rotting in the sun.)

Big Bessie throws her son into the street

A day of sunny face and temper.
The winter trees
Are musical.

Bright lameness from my beautiful disease,
You have your destiny to chip and eat.

Be precise.
With something better than candles in the eyes.
(Candles are not enough.)

At the root of the will, a wild inflammable stuff.

New pioneer of days and ways, be gone.
Hunt out your own or make your own alone.

Go down the street.

In the Mecca

1968

To the memory of Langston Hughes;
and to James Baldwin, Amiri Baraka,
and Mike Alexandroff,
educators extraordinaire

IN THE MECCA

". . . a great gray hulk of brick, four stories high, topped by an ungainly smokestack, ancient and enormous, filling half the block north of Thirty-fourth Street between State and Dearborn . . . the Mecca Building. . . . The Mecca Building is U-shaped. The dirt courtyard is littered with newspapers and tin cans, milk cartons and broken glass. . . . Iron fire escapes run up the building's face and ladders reach from them to the roof. There are four main entrances, two on Dearborn and two on State Street. At each is a gray stone threshold and over each is carved 'THE MECCA.' (The Mecca was constructed as an apartment building in 1891, a splendid palace, a showplace of Chicago. . . .)"

—JOHN BARTLOW MARTIN

"How many people live here? . . . Two thousand? oh, more than that. There's 176 apartments and some of 'em's got seven rooms and they're all full."

—A MECCAN

". . . there's danger in my neighborhood. . . ."

—RICHARD "PEANUT" WASHINGTON

"There comes a time when what has been can never be again."

—RUSS MEEK

IN TRIBUTE—

Jim Cunningham, Jim Taylor, Mike Cook,
Walter Bradford, Don Lee, Curtis Ellis,
Roy Lewis, Peggy Susberry, Ronda Davis,
Carolyn Rodgers, Sharon Scott,
Alicia Johnson, Jewel Latimore

Now the way of the Mecca was on this wise.

Sit where the light corrupts your face.
Miës Van der Rohe retires from grace.
And the fair fables fall.

S. Smith is Mrs. Sallie. Mrs. Sallie
hies home to Mecca, hies to marvelous rest;
ascends the sick and influential stair.
The eye unrinsed, the mouth absurd
with the last sourings of the master's Feast.
She plans
to set severity apart,
to unclench the heavy folly of the fist.
Infirm booms
and suns that have not spoken die behind this
low-brown butterball. Our prudent partridge.
A fragmentary attar and armed coma.
A fugitive attar and a district hymn.

Sees old St. Julia Jones, who has had prayer,
and who is rising from amenable knees

inside the wide-flung door of 215.
"Isn't He wonderfulwonderful!" cries St. Julia.
"Isn't our Lord the greatest to the brim?
The light of my life. And I lie late
past the still pastures. And meadows. He's the comfort
and wine and piccalilli for my soul.
He hunts me up the coffee for my cup.
Oh how I love that Lord."

And Mrs. Sallie,

all innocent of saints and signatures,
nods and consents, content to endorse
Lord as an incense and a vintage. Speaks
to Prophet Williams, young beyond St. Julia,
and rich with Bible, pimples, pout: who reeks
with lust for his disciple, is an engine
of candid steel hugging combustibles.
His wife she was a skeleton.
His wife she was a bone.
Ida died in self-defense.
(Kinswomen!
Kinswomen!)
Ida died alone.

Out of her dusty threshold bursts Hyena.
The striking debutante. A fancier of firsts.
One of the first, and to the tune of hate,
in all the Mecca to paint her hair sun-gold.

And Mrs.

Sallie sees Alfred. Ah, his God!—
To create! To create! To bend with the tight intentness
over the neat detail, come to
a terrified standstill of the heart, then shiver,

then rush—successfully—
at that rebuking thing, that obstinate and
recalcitrant little beast, the phrase!
To have the joy of deciding—successfully—
how stuffs can be compounded or sifted out
and emphasized; what the importances are;
what coats in which to wrap things. Alfred is un-
talented. Knows. Marks time and themes at Phillips,
stares, glares, of mornings, at a smear
which does not care what he may claim or doubt
or probe or clear or want, or what he might have been.
He "fails" no one; at faculty lunch hour
allows the zoology teacher, who has great legs,
to fondle him and curse his pretty hair. He
reads Shakespeare in the evenings or reads Joyce
or James or Horace, Huxley, Hemingway.
Later, he goes to bed with Telly Bell
in 309, or with that golden girl,
or thinks, or drinks until the Everything
is vaguely a part of One thing and the One thing
delightfully anonymous
and undiscoverable. So he is weak,
is weak, is no good. Never mind.
It is a decent enough no-goodness. And it is
a talkative, curly, charitable, spiced weakness
which makes a woman in charge of zoology
dream furiously at night.
When there were all those gods
administering to panthers,
jumping over mountains,
and lighting stars and comets and a moon,
what was their one Belief?

what was their joining thing?

A boy breaks glass and Mrs. Sallie
rises to the final and fourth floor.

Children, what she has brought you is hock of ham.
She puts the pieces to boil in white enamel, right
already with water of many seasonings, at the back
of the cruel stove. And mustard mesmerized by
eldest daughter, the Undaunted (she who once
pushed her thumbs in the eyes of a Thief), awaits
the clever hand. Six ruddy yams abide, and
cornbread made with water.

Now Mrs. Sallie
confers her bird-hat to her kitchen table,
and sees her kitchen. It is bad, is bad,
her eyes say, and My soft antagonist,
her eyes say, and My headlong tax and mote,
her eyes say, and My maniac default,
my least light.
"But all my lights are little!"
Her denunciation
slaps savagely not only this sick kitchen but
her Lord's annulment of the main event.
"I want to decorate!" But what is that? A
pomade atop a sewage. An offense.
First comes correctness, *then* embellishment!
And music, mode, and mixed philosophy
may follow fitly on propriety
to tame the whiskey of our discontent!
"What can I do?"
        But World (a sheep)

wants to be Told.
If you ask a question, you
can't stop there.
You must keep going.
You can't stop there: World will
waive; will be
facetious, angry. You can't stop there.
You have to keep on going.

Doublemint as a protective device. Yvonne
prepares for her lover.
Gum is something he can certify.
Gum is something he can understand.
A tough girl gets it. A rough
Ruthie or Sue. It is unembarrassable,
and will seem likely. It is very bad,
but in its badness it is nearly grand,
and is a crown that tops bald innocence
and gentle fright.
It is not necessary, says Yvonne,
to have every day him whom
to the end thereof you will love.
Because it is tasty to remember
he is alive, and laughs
in somebody else's room,
or is slicing a cold cucumber,
or is buttoning his cuffs,
or is signing with his pen
and will plan
to touch you again.

Melodie Mary hates everything pretty and plump.
And Melodie, Cap and Casey

and Thomas Earl, Tennessee, Emmett and Briggs
hate sewn suburbs;
hate everything combed and strong; hate people who
have balls, dolls, mittens and dimity frocks and trains
and boxing gloves, picture books, bonnets for Easter.
Lace handkerchief owners are enemies of Smithkind.

Melodie Mary likes roaches,
and pities the gray rat.
To delicate Melodie Mary
headlines are secondary.
It is interesting that in China
the children blanch and scream,
and that blood runs like a ragged wound
through the ancient flesh of the land.
It matters, mildly,
that the Chinese girls are grim,
and that hurried are the seizures
of yellow hand on hand. . . .
What if they drop like the tumbling tears
of the old and intelligent sky?
Where are the frantic bulletins
when other importances die?
Trapped in his privacy of pain
the worried rat expires,
and smashed in the grind of a rapid heel
last night's roaches lie.

Briggs is adult as a stone
(who if he cries cries alone).
The Gangs are out, but he must go
to and fro,
appease what reticences move

across the intemperate range.
Immunity is forfeit, love
is luggage, hope is heresy.
Gang
is health and mange.
Gang
is a bunch of ones and a singlicity.
Please pity Briggs. But there is a central height in pity
past which man's hand and sympathy cannot go;
past which the little hurt dog
descends to mass—no longer Joe,
not Bucky, not Cap'n, not Rex,
not Briggs—and is all self-employed,
concerned with Other,
not with Us.
Briggs, how "easy," finally, to accept (after the shriek and
repulsion)
the unacceptable evil. To proceed with some éclat;
some salvation of the face;
awake! to choke the chickens, file their blood.

One reason cats are happier than people
is that they have no newspapers . . . I must be,
culls Tennessee,
like my cat, content to gaze
at men and women spurting here and there.
I must sit, let
them stroke me as and when they will;
must drink their milk and cry
for meat. At other times I must be still.
Who tingles in
and mixes with affairs and others met
comes out with scratches and is very thin

and rides the red possession of regret.

In the midst
of hells and gruels and little halloweens
tense Thomas Earl loves Johnny Appleseed.
"I, Johnny Appleseed."
It is hard to be Johnny Appleseed.
The ground shudders.
The ground springs up;
hits you with gnarls and rust,
derangement and fever, or blare and clerical treasons.

Emmett and Cap and Casey
are skin wiped over bones
for lack of chub and chocolate
and ice cream cones,
for lack of English muffins
and boysenberry jam.
What shall their redeemer be?
Greens and hock of ham.
For each his greens and hock of ham
and a spoon of sweet potato.

Alfred says:
The faithless world!
betraying yet again
trinities!
My chaste displeasure
is not enough;
the brilliant British of the new command
is not enough;
the counsels of division, the hot counsels,

the scuffle and short pout
are not enough, are only
a pressure of clankings and affinities
against
the durable fictions of a Charming Trash.
Mrs. Sallie
evokes and loves and loathes a pink-lit image
of the toy-child. Her Lady's.
Her Lady's pink convulsion, toy-child dances
in stiff wide pink through Mrs. Sallie. Stiff pink is
on toy-child's poverty of cream
under a shiny tended warp of gold.
What shiny tended gold is an aubade
for toy-child's head! Has ribbons too!
Ribbons. Not Woolworth cotton comedy,
not rubber band, not string. . . .
"And that would be my baby be my baby. . . .
And I would be my lady I my lady. . . ."

What else is there to say but everything?

SUDDENLY, COUNTING NOSES, MRS. SALLIE
SEES NO PEPITA. "WHERE PEPITA BE?"

. . . Cap, where Pepita? Casey, where Pepita?
Emmett and Melodie Mary, where Pepita?
Briggs, Tennessee, Yvonne, and Thomas Earl,
where may our Pepita be?—
our Woman with her terrible eye,
with iron and feathers in her feet,
with all her songs so lemon-sweet,
with lightning and a candle too

and junk and jewels too?
My heart begins to race.
I fear the end of Peace.

Ain seen er I ain seen er I ain seen er
Ain seen er I ain seen er I ain seen er

Yvonne up-ends her iron. And is constrained.
Cannot now conjure love-within-the-park.
Cannot now conjure spice and soft explosion
mixing with miffed mosquitoes where the dark
defines and re-defines.

And Melodie Mary
and Thomas Earl and Tennessee and Briggs
yield cat-contentment gangs rats Appleseed.

Emmett and Cap and Casey
yield visions of vice and veal,
dimes and windy carnival,
candied orange peel,
peppermint in a pickle;
and where the ladybug
glistens in her leaf-hammock; *light*
lasses to hiss and hug.

And they are constrained. All are constrained.
And there is no thinking of grapes or gold
or of any wicked sweetness and they ride
upon fright and remorse and their stomachs
are rags or grit.
In twos!
In threes! Knock-knocking down the martyred halls

at doors behind whose yelling oak or pine
　　many flowers start, choke, reach up,
　　want help, get it, do not get it,
　　rally, bloom, or die on the wasting vine.

"One of my children is missing. One of my children is gone."

Great-great Gram hobbles, fumbles at the knob,
mumbles, "I ain seen no Pepita. But
I remember our cabin. The floor was dirt.
And something crawled in it. That is the thought
stays in my mind. I do not recollect
what 'twas. But something. Something creebled in that dirt
for we wee ones to pop. Kept popping at it.
Something that squishied. *Then* your heel come down!
I hear them squishies now. . . . *Pop*, Pernie May!
That's sister Pernie. That's my sister Pernie.
Squish. . . . Out would jump her little heel.
And that was the end of Something. Sister Pernie
was our best popper. Pern and me and all,
we had no beds. Some slaves had beds of hay
or straw, with cover-cloth. We six-uns curled
in corners of the dirt, and closed our eyes,
and went to sleep—or listened to the rain
fall inside, felt the drops
big on our noses, bummies and tum-tums. . . ."

Although he has not seen Pepita, Loam
Norton considers Belsen and Dachau,
regrets all old unkindnesses and harms.
. . . The Lord was their shepherd.
Yet did they want.
Joyfully would they have lain in jungles or pastures,

walked beside waters. Their gaunt
souls were not restored, their souls were banished.
In the shadow valley
they feared the evil, whether with or without God.
They were comforted by no Rod,
no Staff, but flayed by, O besieged by, shot a-plenty.
The prepared table was the rot or curd of the day.
Anointings were of lice. Blood was the spillage of cups.
Goodness and mercy should follow them
    all the days of their death.
They should dwell in the house of the Lord forever
and, dwelling, save a place for me.
I am not remote,
not unconcerned. . . .

Boontsie De Broe has
not seen Pepita Smith: but is
a Lady
among Last Ladies.
Erect. Direct.
An engraving on the crowd, the blurred crowd.
She is away and fond.
Her clear voice tells you life may be controlled.
Her clear mind is the extract
of massive literatures, of lores,
transactions of old ocean; suffrages.

Yvonne
recovers to aver
despite the stomp of the stupor.
    She will not go
in Hudson's hashhouse. And the Tivoli
is a muffler of Love.

In the blasé park,
that winks and mocks but is at all times
tolerant of the virtuous defect, of audit,
        and of mangle and of wile, he
may permit perusal of their ground,
its rubble-over-rose: may look to rainbow:
may sanction bridal tulle, white flowers,
may allow a mention of a minister and twins. . . .

        But *other* Smiths are twitching. They recall
vain vagrants, recall old peddlers, young fine bumlets,
The Man Who Sells The Peaches Plums Bananas.
They recall the Fuller Brush Man,
oblique and delicate, who tries on
the very fit and feature of despair.
"Pepita's smart," says Sallie; her stretched eyes
reject the exact despatches of a mind turned boiler,
epithet, foiler, guillotine. *What*
of the Bad Old Man? the lover-like young man? the
half-mad boy who put his hand across Pepita's knee?
"Pepita's smart," says Sallie.
Knowing the ham hocks are burning at the bottom of the pan.

S. and eight of her children reach their door. The
door says, "What are you doing here? and where
is Pepita the puny—the halted, glad-sad child?"
They pet themselves, subdue
the legislation of their yoke and devils.
                Has just wandered!
                Has just blundered
                away
                from her own.
                And there's no worry

that's necessary.
She
comes soon alone.
Comes soon alone or will be brought by neighbor.
Kind neighbor.

"Kind neighbor." They consider.
Suddenly
every one in the world is Mean.
Could that old woman, passively passing, mash a child?
Has she a tot's head in that shiny bag?
And that lank fellow looking furtive.
What
cold poison could he spew, what stench commit
upon a little girl, a little lost girl,
lone and languid in the world, wanting
her ma, her glad-sad, her Yvonne?

Emmett runs down the hall.
Emmett seizes John Tom's telephone.
(Despite the terror and the derivation,
despite the not avuncular frontier,
John Tom, twice forty in 420, claims
Life sits or blazes in this Mecca.
And thereby—tenable.
And thereby beautiful.)

Provoking calm and dalliance of the Law.
How shall the Law allow for littleness!
How shall the Law enchief the chapters of
wee brown-black chime, wee brown-black chastity?

The Law arrives—and does not quickly go

to fetch a Female of the Negro Race.
A lariat of questions.
The mother screams and wants her baby. Wants her baby,
and wants her baby wants her baby.

Law leaves, with likeness of a "southern" belle. Sheriffs,
South State Street is a Postulate!
Until you look. You look—and you discover
the paper dolls are terrible. You touch.
You look and touch.
The paper dolls are terrible and cold.

Aunt Dill arrives to help them. "Little gal got
raped and choked to death last week. Her gingham
was tied around her neck and it was red
but had been green before with pearls and dots
of rhinestone on the collar, and her tongue
was hanging out (a little to the side);
her eye was all a-pop, one was; was one
all gone. Part of her little nose was gone
(bit off, the Officer said). The Officer said
that something not quite right been done that girl.
Lived Langley: 'round the corner from my house."
Aunt Dill extends
sinister pianissimos and apples,
and at that moment of the Thousand Souls is
a Christ-like creature, Doing Good.

The Law returns. It trots about the Mecca.
It pounds a dozen doors.

No, Alfred has not seen Pepita Smith.
But he (who might have been an architect)

can speak of Mecca: firm arms surround
disorders, bruising ruses and small hells,
small semiheavens: hug barbarous rhetoric
built of buzz, coma and petite pell-mells.
No, Alfred has not seen Pepita Smith.
But he (who might have been a poet-king)
can speak superbly of the line of Leopold.
The line of Leopold is thick with blackness
 and Scriptural drops and rises.
The line of Leopold is busy with betrothals of royal rage
 and conditional pardon and with
refusal of mothballs for outmoded love.
Senghor will not shred
love,
gargantuan gardens careful in the sun,
fairy story gold, thrones, feasts, the three princesses,
summer sailboats
like cartoon ghosts or Klansmen, pointing up
white questions, in blue air. . . .
No.
Believes in beauty.
But believes that blackness is among the fit filters.
Old cobra
coughs and curdles in his lungs,
spits spite, spits exquisite spite, and cries, "Ignoble!"
Needs "negritude."
Senghor (in Europe rootless and lonely) sings in art-lines
of Black Woman.
Senghor sighs and, "negritude" needing,
speaks for others, for brothers. Alfred can tell of
Poet, and muller, and President of Senegal, who
in voice and body

loves sun,
listens
to the rich pound in and beneath the black feet of Africa.

Hyena, the striking debutante, is back;
bathed, used by special oils and fumes, will be
off to the Ball tonight. She has not seen
Pepita—"a puny and a putrid little child."

Death is easy.
It may come quickly.
It may come when nobody is ready.
Death may come at any time. Mazola
has never known Pepita S. but knows
the strangest thing is when the stretcher goes!—
the elegant hucksters bearing the body when the body
leaves its late lair the last time leaves.
With no plans for return.

Don Lee wants
not a various America.
Don Lee wants
a new nation
under nothing;
a physical light that waxes; he does not want to
be exorcised, adjoining and revered;
he does not like a local garniture
nor any impish onus in the vogue;
is not candlelit
but stands out in the auspices of fire
and rock and jungle-flail;
wants

new art and anthem; will
want a new music screaming in the sun.

Says Alfred:
To be a red bush!
In the West Virginia autumn.
To flame out red.
"Crimson" is not word enough,
although close to what I mean.
How proud.
How proud.
(But the bush does not know it flames.)

"Takes time," grated the gradualist.
"Starting from when?" asked Amos.
Amos (not Alfred) says,
"Shall we sit on ourselves; shall we wait behind roses and veils
for monsters to maul us,
        for bulls to come butt us forever and ever,
shall we scratch in our blood,
        point air-powered hands at our wounds,
reflect on the aim of our bulls?" And Amos
(not Alfred) prays, for America prays:
"Bathe her in her beautiful blood.
A long blood bath will wash her pure.
Her skin needs special care.
Let this good rage continue out beyond
her power to believe or to surmise.
Slap the false sweetness from that face.
Great-nailed boots
must kick her prostrate, heel-grind that soft breast,
outrage her saucy pride,
remove her fair fine mask.

Let her lie there, panting and wild, her pain
red, running roughly through the illustrious ruin—
with nothing to do but think, think
of how she was so long grand,
flogging her dark one with her own hand,
watching in meek amusement while he bled.
Then shall she rise, recover.
Never to forget."

The ballad of Edie Barrow:
I fell in love with a Gentile boy.
All creamy-and-golden fair.
He looked deep and long in my long black eyes.
And he played with my long black hair.
He took me away to his summertime house.
He was wondrous wealthy, was he.
And there in the hot black drapes of night
he whispered, "Good lovers are we."
Close was our flesh through the winking hours,
closely and sweetly entwined.
Love did not guess in the tight-packed dark
it was flesh of varying kind.
Scarletly back when the hateful sun
came bragging across the town.
And I could have killed the gentle Gentile
who waited to strap him down.
He will wed her come fall, come falling of fall.
And she will be queen of his rest.
I shall be queen of his summerhouse storm.
A hungry tooth in my breast.

"Pepita who?" And Prophet Williams yawns.
Prophet Williams' office in the Mecca

has a soiled window and a torn front sign.
His suit is shabby and slick.
He is not poor (clothes do *not* make the man).
He has a lawyer named Enrico Jason,
who talks. The Prophet advertises
in every Colored journal in the world. . . .
An old woman wants
from the most reverend Prophet of all prophets
a piece of cloth, licked by his Second Tongue,
to wrap around her paralytic leg.
Men with malicious sweethearts, evil sweethearts—
bringers of bad, bringers of tedium—
want Holy Thunderbolts, and Love Balls too.
And all want lucky numbers all the time.
Mallie (the Superintendent of six secretaries)
types. Mallie alone may know
the Combinations:
14–15–16
and 13–14–15. . . .
(magic is Cut-out Number Forty-three).
Prophet will help you hold your Job, solve problems,
and, like a Sister Stella in Blue Island,
"can call your friends and enemies by name
without a single clue."
There is no need to visit in Blue Island.
Prophet will give you trading stamps and kisses,
or a cigar.
One visit will convince you.
Lucky days
and Lucky Hands. Lifts you
from Sorrow and the Shadows. Heals the body.
A Sister Marlo on east Sixty-third
announces One

Visit Can Keep You Out of the Insane Asylum,
but
she stocks no Special Holiday Blessings for
Columbus Day and Christmas, nor keeps off
green devils and orange witches with striped fangs.
Prophet
has Drawing and Holding Powder, Attraction Powder, Black
Cat Powder, Powerful Serum,
"Marvelous Potency Number Ninety-one"
(which stoppeth husbands and lovers from dastardy),
Pay-check Fluid, Running-around Elixir,
Policy Number Compeller, Voodoo Potion.
Enrico Jason, a glossy circular blackness, who
sees Lawmen and enhances Lawmen, soon
will lie beside his Prophet in bright blood,
a rhythm of stillness
above the nuances.

How many care, Pepita?—
Staley and Lara,
the victim grasped, the harlot had and gone?
Eunie, the intimate tornado?
Simpson, the peasant king, Bixby and June,
the hollowed, the scant, the
played-out deformities? the margins?
Not those.
Not these three Maries
with warm unwary mouths and asking eyes
wide open, full of vagueness and surprise;
the limp ladies
(two in awful combat now:
a terrible battle of the Old:
speechless and physical: oh horrible

the obscene gruntings
the dull outwittings
the flabby semi-rhythmic shufflings
the blear starings
the small spittings).
Not Great-uncle Beer, white-headed twinkly man!—
laugher joker gambler killer too.
Great-uncle Beer says, "Casey Jones.
Yes, Casey Jones is still alive,
a chicken on his head."
Not Wezlyn, the wandering woman, the woman who wander
the halls of the Mecca at night, in search
of Lawrence and Love.

Not Insane Sophie! If
you scream, you're marked "insane."
But silence is a *place* in which to scream!
Hush.
An agitation in the bush.
Occluded trees.
Mad life heralding the blue heat of God
snickers in a corner of the west windowsill.
"What have I done, and to the world,
and to the love I promised Mother?"
An agitation in occluded trees.
The fires run up. Things slant.
The pillow's wet.
The fires run down and flatten.
(The grilles will dance over glass!)
You're marked "insane."
You cower.
Suddenly you're no longer
well-dressed. You're not
pretty in halls.

Like the others you want love, but
a cage is imminent.
Your doll is near. And will go with you.
Your doll, whom none will stun.

. . . How many care, Pepita?
Does Darkara?
Darkara looks at *Vogue*. Darkara sees
a mischievous impromptu and a sheen.
(In Palm Beach, Florida, Laddie Sanford says:
"I call it My Ocean. Of course, it's the Atlantic.")
The painter, butcher, stockyards man, the Typist,
Aunt Tippie, Zombie Bell,
Mr. Kelly with long gray hair who begs
subtly from door to door, Gas Cady
the man who robbed J. Harrison's grave of mums
and left the peony bush only because
it was too big (said Mama), the janitor
who is a Political Person, Queenie King who
is an old poem silvering the noise,
and Wallace Williams who knows the
Way the Thing Is Supposed To Be Done—
these little care, Pepita, what befalls a
nullified saint or forfeiture (or child).

Alfred's Impression—his Apologie—
his Invocation—and his Ecstasie:
"Not Baudelaire, Bob Browning, not Neruda.
Giants over Steeples
are wanted in this Crazy-eyes, this Scar.
A violent reverse.
We part from all we thought we knew of love
and of dismay-with-flags-on. What we know

is that there are confusion and conclusion.
Rending.
Even the hardest parting is a contribution. . . .
What shall we say?
Farewell. And Hail! Until Farewell again."

Officers!—
do you nearly wish you had not come into this room?
The sixtyish sisters, the twins with the floured faces,
who dress in long stiff blackness,
who exit stiffly together and enter together
stiffly,
muffle their Mahler, finish their tea,
stare at the lips of the Law—
but have not seen Pepita anywhere.
They pull on their long white gloves,
they flour their floured faces,
and stiffly leave Law and the Mecca.

Way-out Morgan is collecting guns
in a tiny fourth-floor room.
He is not hungry, ever, though sinfully lean.
He flourishes, ever, on porridge or pat of bean
pudding or wiener soup—fills fearsomely
on visions of Death-to-the-Hordes-of-the-White-Men!
Death!
(This is the Maxim painted in big black
above a bed bought at a Champlain rummage sale.)
Remembering three local-and-legal beatings, he
rubs his hands in glee,
does Way-out Morgan. Remembering his Sister
mob-raped in Mississippi, Way-out Morgan
smacks sweet his lips and adds another gun

and listens to Blackness stern and blunt and beautiful,
organ-rich Blackness telling a terrible story.
Way-out Morgan
predicts the Day of Debt-pay shall begin,
the Day of Demon-diamond,
of blood in mouths and body-mouths,
of flesh-rip in the Forum of Justice at last!
Remembering mates in the Mississippi River,
mates with black bodies once majestic, Way-out
postpones a yellow woman in his bed, postpones
wetnesses and little cries and stomachings—
to consider Ruin.

"Pepita? No."
Marian is mixing.
Take Marian mixing. Gumbo File or roux.
At iron: at ire with faucet, husband, young.
Knows no
gold hour.
Sings
but sparsely, and subscribes to axioms
atop her gargoyles and tamed foam. Good axioms.
Craves crime: her murder, her deep wounding, or
a leprosy so lovely as to pop
the slights and sleep of her community,
her Mecca.
A Thing. To make the people heel and stop
and See her.
Never strides
about, up!
Never alters earth or air!
Her children cannot quake, be proud.
Her husband never Saw her, never said

her single silver certain Self aloud.

Pops Pinkham, forgetting Pepita,
is somewhat doubtful of a specific right
to inherit the earth or to partake of it now....

Old women should not seek to be perfumed, said Plutarch.
But Dill, the kind of woman you
peek at in passing and thank your God or zodiac you
may never have to know, puts on *Tabu.*
Aunt Dill is happy. Nine years Little Papa
has been completely at rest in Lincoln Cemetery.
Children were stillbirths all. Aunt Dill
has bits of brass and marble, and Franciscan
china; has crocheted doilies; has old mahogany,
polished till it burns with a smothered glow; has
antimacassars, spreads, silk draperies,
her silver creamer and her iron lamp,
her piece of porcelain, her seventeen
Really Nice handkerchiefs pressed in cedar. Dill
is woman-in-love-with-God.
Is not
true-child-of-God—for are we ever to
be children?—are we never to mature,
be lovely lovely? be soft Woman
rounded and darling . . . almost caressable . . .
and certainly wearing *Tabu* in the name of the Lord.
Dill straightens—tries to forget the hand of God
(. . . which would be skillful . . . would be flattering . . .)

I hate it.
Yet, murmurs Alfred—

who is lean at the balcony, leaning—
something, something in Mecca
continues to call! Substanceless; yet like mountains,
like rivers and oceans too; and like trees
with wind whistling through them. And steadily
an essential sanity, black and electric,
builds to a reportage and redemption.
        A hot estrangement.
        A material collapse
that is Construction.

Hateful things sometimes befall the hateful
but the hateful are not rendered lovable thereby.
The murderer of Pepita
looks at the Law unlovably. Jamaican
Edward denies and thrice denies a dealing
of any dimension with Mrs. Sallie's daughter.
        Beneath his cot
a little woman lies in dust with roaches.
She never went to kindergarten.
She never learned that black is not beloved.
Was royalty when poised,
sly, at the A and P's fly-open door.
Will be royalty no more.
"I touch"—she said once—"petals of a rose.
A silky feeling through me goes!"
Her mother will try for roses.

She whose little stomach fought the world had
wriggled, like a robin!
Odd were the little wrigglings
and the chopped chirpings oddly rising.

AFTER MECCA

TO A WINTER SQUIRREL

That is the way God made you.
And what is wrong with it? Why, nothing.
Except that you are cold and cannot cook.

Merdice can cook. Merdice
of murdered heart and docked sarcastic soul,
Merdice
the bolted nomad, on a winter noon
cooks guts; and sits in gas. (She has no shawl, her
landlord has no coal.)

You out beyond the shellac of her look
and of her sill!
She envies you your furry
buffoonery
that enfolds your silver skill.
She thinks you are a mountain and a star, unbaffleable;
with sentient twitch and scurry.

BOY BREAKING GLASS

To Marc Crawford
from whom the commissioin

Whose broken window is a cry of art
(success, that winks aware
as elegance, as a treasonable faith)
is raw: is sonic: is old-eyed première.
Our beautiful flaw and terrible ornament.
Our barbarous and metal little man.

"I shall create! If not a note, a hole.
If not an overture, a desecration."

Full of pepper and light
and Salt and night and cargoes.

"Don't go down the plank
if you see there's no extension.
Each to his grief, each to
his loneliness and fidgety revenge.

Nobody knew where I was and now I am no longer there."

The only sanity is a cup of tea.
The music is in minors.

Each one other
is having different weather.

"It was you, it was you who threw away my name!
And this is everything I have for me."

Who has not Congress, lobster, love, luau,
the Regency Room, the Statue of Liberty,
runs. A sloppy amalgamation.
A mistake.
A cliff.
A hymn, a snare, and an exceeding sun.

MEDGAR EVERS

For Charles Evers

The man whose height his fear improved he
arranged to fear no further. The raw
intoxicated time was time for better birth or
a final death.

Old styles, old tempos, all the engagement of
the day—the sedate, the regulated fray—
the antique light, the Moral rose, old gusts,
tight whistlings from the past, the mothballs
in the Love at last our man forswore.

Medgar Evers annoyed confetti and assorted
brands of businessmen's eyes.

The shows came down: to maxims and surprise.
And palsy.

Roaring no rapt arise-ye to the dead, he
leaned across tomorrow. People said that
he was holding clean globes in his hands.

MALCOLM X

For Dudley Randall

Original.
Ragged-round.
Rich-robust.

He had the hawk-man's eyes.
We gasped. We saw the maleness.
The maleness raking out and making guttural the air
and pushing us to walls.

And in a soft and fundamental hour
a sorcery devout and vertical
beguiled the world.

He opened us—
who was a key,

who was a man.

TWO DEDICATIONS

I

THE CHICAGO PICASSO

August 15, 1967

> "Mayor Daley tugged a white ribbon, loosing the blue percale wrap. A hearty cheer went up as the covering slipped off the big steel sculpture that looks at once like a bird and a woman."
>
> —Chicago *Sun-Times*

(Seiji Ozawa leads the Symphony.
The Mayor smiles.
And 50,000 See.)

Does man love Art? Man visits Art, but squirms.
Art hurts. Art urges voyages—
and it is easier to stay at home,
the nice beer ready.
      In commonrooms
we belch, or sniff, or scratch.
Are raw.

But we must cook ourselves and style ourselves for Art, who
is a requiring courtesan.
We squirm.
We do not hug the Mona Lisa.
We
may touch or tolerate
an astounding fountain, or a horse-and-rider.

At most, another Lion.

Observe the tall cold of a Flower
which is as innocent and as guilty,
as meaningful and as meaningless as any
other flower in the western field.

II

THE WALL

August 27, 1967

For Edward Christmas

"The side wall of a typical slum building on the corner of 43rd and Langley became a mural communicating black dignity. . . ."

—*Ebony*

A drumdrumdrum.
Humbly we come.
South of success and east of gloss and glass are
sandals;
flowercloth;
grave hoops of wood or gold, pendant
from black ears, brown ears, reddish-brown
and ivory ears;

black boy-men.
Black
boy-men on roofs fist out "Black Power!" Val,
a little black stampede
in African
images of brass and flowerswirl,
fists out "Black Power!"—tightens pretty eyes,
leans back on mothercountry and is tract,
is treatise through her perfect and tight teeth.

Women in wool hair chant their poetry.

Phil Cohran gives us messages and music
made of developed bone and polished and honed cult.
It is the Hour of tribe and of vibration,
the day-long Hour. It is the Hour
of ringing, rouse, of ferment-festival.

On Forty-third and Langley
black furnaces resent ancient
legislatures
of ploy and scruple and practical gelatin.
They keep the fever in,
fondle the fever.

All
worship the Wall.

I mount the rattling wood. Walter
says, "She is good." Says, "She
our Sister is." In front of me
hundreds of faces, red-brown, brown, black, ivory,
yield me hot trust, their yea and their Announcement
that they are ready to rile the high-flung ground.
Behind me, Paint.
Heroes.
No child has defiled
the Heroes of this Wall this serious Appointment
this still Wing
this Scald this Flute this heavy Light this Hinge.

An emphasis is paroled.
The old decapitations are revised,
the dispossessions beakless.

And we sing.

THE BLACKSTONE RANGERS

I

AS SEEN BY DISCIPLINES

There they are.
Thirty at the corner.
Black, raw, ready.
Sores in the city
that do not want to heal.

II

THE LEADERS

Jeff. Gene. Geronimo. And Bop.
They cancel, cure and curry.
Hardly the dupes of the downtown thing
the cold bonbon,
the rhinestone thing. And hardly
in a hurry.
Hardly Belafonte, King,
Black Jesus, Stokely, Malcolm X or Rap.
Bungled trophies.
Their country is a Nation on no map.

Jeff, Gene, Geronimo and Bop
in the passionate noon,
in bewitching night
are the detailed men, the copious men.
They curry, cure,
they cancel, cancelled images whose Concerts
are not divine, vivacious; the different tins
are intense last entries; pagan argument;

translations of the night.

The Blackstone bitter bureaus
(bureaucracy is footloose) edit, fuse
unfashionable damnations and descent;
and exulting, monstrous hand on monstrous hand,
construct, strangely, a monstrous pearl or grace.

III

GANG GIRLS

A Rangerette

Gang Girls are sweet exotics.
Mary Ann
uses the nutrients of her orient,
but sometimes sighs for Cities of blue and jewel
beyond her Ranger rim of Cottage Grove.
(Bowery Boys, Disciples, Whip-Birds will
dissolve no margins, stop no savory sanctities.)

Mary is
a rose in a whiskey glass.

Mary's
Februaries shudder and are gone. Aprils
fret frankly, lilac hurries on.
Summer is a hard irregular ridge.
October looks away.
And that's the Year!
                    Save for her bugle-love.
Save for the bleat of not-obese devotion.

Save for Somebody Terribly Dying, under
the philanthropy of robins. Save for her Ranger
bringing
an amount of rainbow in a string-drawn bag.
"Where did you get the diamond?" Do not ask:
but swallow, straight, the spirals of his flask
and assist him at your zipper; pet his lips
and help him clutch you.

Love's another departure.
Will there be any arrivals, confirmations?
Will there be gleaning?

Mary, the Shakedancer's child
from the rooming-flat, pants carefully, peers at
her laboring lover. . . .
                    Mary! Mary Ann!
Settle for sandwiches! settle for stocking caps!
for sudden blood, aborted carnival,
the props and niceties of non-loneliness—
the rhymes of Leaning.

THE SERMON ON THE WARPLAND

"The fact that we are black
is our ultimate reality."
—Ron Karenga

And several strengths from drowsiness campaigned
but spoke in Single Sermon on the warpland.

And went about the warpland saying No.
"My people, black and black, revile the River.
Say that the River turns, and turn the River.

Say that our Something in doublepod contains
seeds for the coming hell and health together.
Prepare to meet
(sisters, brothers) the brash and terrible weather;
the pains;
the bruising; the collapse of bestials, idols.
But then oh then!—the stuffing of the hulls!
the seasoning of the perilously sweet!
the health! the heralding of the clear obscure!

Build now your Church, my brothers, sisters. Build

never with brick nor Corten nor with granite.
Build with lithe love. With love like lion-eyes.
With love like morningrise.
With love like black, our black—
luminously indiscreet;
complete; continuous."

THE SECOND SERMON ON THE WARPLAND

For Walter Bradford

1.

This is the urgency: Live!
and have your blooming in the noise of the whirlwind.

2.

Salve salvage in the spin.
Endorse the splendor splashes;
stylize the flawed utility;
prop a malign or failing light—
but know the whirlwind is our commonwealth.
Not the easy man, who rides above them all,
not the jumbo brigand,
not the pet bird of poets, that sweetest sonnet,
shall straddle the whirlwind.
Nevertheless, live.

3.

All about are the cold places,
all about are the pushmen and jeopardy, theft—
all about are the stormers and scramblers but
what must our Season be, which starts from Fear?
Live and go out.
Define and
medicate the whirlwind.

4.

The time
cracks into furious flower. Lifts its face
all unashamed. And sways in wicked grace.
Whose half-black hands assemble oranges
is tom-tom hearted
(goes in bearing oranges and boom).
And there are bells for orphans—
and red and shriek and sheen.
A garbageman is dignified
as any diplomat.
Big Bessie's feet hurt like nobody's business,
but she stands—bigly—under the unruly scrutiny, stands in the
wild weed.

In the wild weed
she is a citizen,
and is a moment of highest quality; admirable.

It is lonesome, yes. For we are the last of the loud.
Nevertheless, live.

Conduct your blooming in the noise and whip of the whirlwind.

from
Primer for Blacks

TO THOSE OF MY SISTERS WHO KEPT THEIR NATURALS

Never to look
a hot comb in the teeth.

Sisters!
I love you.
Because you love you.
Because you are erect.
Because you are also bent.
In season, stern, kind.
Crisp, soft—in season.
And you withhold.
And you extend.
And you Step out.
And you go back.
And you extend again.
Your eyes, loud-soft, with crying and
with smiles,
are older than a million years.
And they are young.
You reach, in season.
You subside, in season.
And All
below the richrough righttime of your hair.

You have not bought Blondine.
You have not hailed the hot-comb recently.
You never worshipped Marilyn Monroe.
You say: Farrah's hair is hers.
You have not wanted to be white.
Nor have you testified to adoration of that
state
with the advertisement of imitation
(*never* successful because the hot-comb is
laughing too.)

But oh the rough dark Other music!
the Real,
the Right.
The natural Respect of Self and Seal!
Sisters!
Your hair is Celebration in the world!

from Beckonings

HORSES GRAZE

Cows graze.
Horses graze.
They
eat
eat
eat.
Their graceful heads
are bowed
bowed
bowed
in majestic oblivion.
They are nobly oblivious
to your follies,
your inflation,
the knocks and nettles of administration.
They
eat
eat
eat.
And at the crest of their brute satisfaction,
with wonderful gentleness, in affirmation,
they lift their clean calm eyes and they lie down

and love the world.
They speak with their companions.
They do not wish that they were otherwhere.
Perhaps they know that creature feet may press
only a few earth inches at a time,
that earth is anywhere earth,
that an eye may see,
wherever it may be,
the Immediate arc, alone, of life, of love.
In Sweden,
China,
Afrika,
in India or Maine
the animals are sane;
they know and know and know
there's ground below
and sky
up high.

A BLACK WEDDING SONG

This love is a rich cry over
the deviltries and the death.
A weapon-song. Keep it strong.

Keep it strong.
Keep it logic and magic and lightning and muscle.

Strong hand in strong hand, stride to
the Assault that is promised you (knowing
no armor assaults a pudding or a mush.)

Here is your Wedding Day.
Here is your launch.

Come to your Wedding Song.

For you
I wish the kindness that romps or sorrows along.
Or kneels.
I wish you the daily forgiveness of each other.
For war comes in from the World
and puzzles a darling duet—

tangles tongues,
tears hearts, mashes minds;
there will be the need to forgive.

I wish you jewels of Black love.
Come to your Wedding Song.

from To Disembark

Riot

RIOT

A Poem in Three Parts

A riot is the language of the unheard.
—Martin Luther King, Jr.

John Cabot, out of Wilma, once a Wycliffe,
all whitebluerose below his golden hair,
wrapped richly in right linen and right wool,
almost forgot his Jaguar and Lake Bluff;
almost forgot Grandtully (which is The
Best Thing That Ever Happened to Scotch); almost
forgot the sculpture at the Richard Gray
and Distelheim; the kidney pie at Maxim's,
the Grenadine de Beouf at Maison Henri.

Because the "Negroes" were coming down the street.

Because the Poor were sweaty and unpretty
(not like Two Dainty Negroes in Winnetka)
and they were coming toward him in rough ranks.
In seas. In windsweep. They were black and loud.
And not detainable. And not discreet.

Gross. Gross. "Que tu es grossier!" John Cabot

itched instantly beneath the nourished white
that told his story of glory to the World.
"Don't let It touch me! the blackness! Lord!" he
whispered to any handy angel in the sky.

But, in a thrilling announcement, on It drove
and breathed on him: and touched him. In that breath
the fume of pig foot, chitterling and cheap chili,
malign, mocked John. And, in terrific touch, old
averted doubt jerked forward decently,
cried "Cabot! John! You are a desperate man,
and the desperate die expensively today."

John Cabot went down in the smoke and fire
and broken glass and blood, and he cried "Lord!
Forgive these nigguhs that know not what they do."

THE THIRD SERMON ON THE WARPLAND

Phoenix:
"In Egyptian mythology,
a bird which lived for five hundred
years and then consumed itself in fire,
rising renewed from the ashes."
—Webster

The earth is a beautiful place.
Watermirrors and things to be reflected.
Goldenrod across the little lagoon.

The Black Philosopher says
"Our chains are in the keep of the keeper
in a labeled cabinet
on the second shelf by the cookies,
sonatas, the arabesques . . .
There's a rattle, sometimes.
You do not hear it who mind only
cookies and crunch them.

You do not hear the remarkable music—'A
Death Song For You Before You Die.'
If you could hear it
you would make music too.
The blackblues."

West Madison Street.
In "Jessie's Kitchen"
nobody's eating Jessie's Perfect Food.
Crazy flowers
cry up across the sky, spreading
and hissing **This is**
it.

The young men run.
They will not steal Bing Crosby but will steal
Melvin Van Peebles who made Lillie
a thing of Zampoughi a thing of red wiggles and trebles
(and I know there are twenty wire stalks sticking out
of her head
as her underfed haunches jerk jazz.)

A clean riot is not one in which little rioters
long-stomped, long-straddled, BEANLESS
but knowing no Why
go steal in hell
a radio, sit to hear James Brown
and Mingus, Young-Holt, Coleman, John,
    on V.O.N.
and sun themselves in Sin.

However, what
is going on
is going on.

Fire.

That is their way of lighting candles in the darkness.
A White Philosopher said
"It is better to light one candle than curse the darkness."
These candles curse—
inverting the deeps of the darkness.

GUARD HERE, GUNS LOADED.

The young men run.
The children in ritual chatter
scatter upon
their Own and old geography.

The Law comes sirening across the town.

A woman is dead.
Motherwoman.
She lies among the boxes
(that held the haughty hat, the Polish sausages)
in newish, thorough, firm virginity
as rich as fudge is if you've had five pieces.
Not again shall she
partake of steak
on Christmas mornings, nor of nighttime
chicken and wine at Val Gray Ward's
nor say
of Mr. Beetley, Exit Jones, Junk Smith
nor neat New-baby Williams (man-to-many)
"He treat me right."

That was a gut gal.

"We'll do an us!" yells Yancey, a twittering twelve.
"Instead of your deathintheafternoon,
kill 'em, bull!
kill 'em, bull!"

The Black Philosopher blares
"I tell you, **exhaustive** black integrity
would assure a blackless America. . . ."

Nine die, Sun-Times will tell
and will tell too
in small black-bordered oblongs **"Rumor? check it
at 744-4111."**

A Poem to Peanut.
"Coooooool!" purrs Peanut. Peanut is
Richard—a Ranger and a gentleman.
A Signature. A Herald. And a Span.
This Peanut will not let his men explode.
And Rico will not.
Neither will Sengali.
Nor Bop nor Jeff, Geronimo nor Lover.
These merely peer and purr,
and pass the Passion over.
The Disciples stir
and thousandfold confer
with ranging Rangermen;
mutual in their "Yeah!—
this AIN'T all upinheah!"

"But WHY do These People offend **themselves**?" say they
who say also "It's time.
It's time to help
These People."

Lies are told and legends made.
Phoenix rises unafraid.

The Black Philosopher will remember:
"There they came to life and exulted,
the hurt mute.
Then it was over.

The dust, as they say, settled."

AN ASPECT OF LOVE, ALIVE IN THE ICE AND FIRE

LaBohem Brown

In a package of minutes there is this We.
How beautiful.
Merry foreigners in our morning,
we laugh, we touch each other,
are responsible props and posts.

A physical light is in the room.

Because the world is at the window
we cannot wonder very long.

You rise. Although
genial, you are in yourself again.
I observe
your direct and respectable stride.
You are direct and self-accepting as a lion
in Afrikan velvet. You are level, lean,
remote.

There is a moment in Camaraderie
when interruption is not to be understood.
I cannot bear an interruption.
This is the shining joy;
the time of not-to-end.

On the street we smile.
We go
in different directions
down the imperturbable street.

Family Pictures

THE LIFE OF LINCOLN WEST

Ugliest little boy
that everyone ever saw.
That is what everyone said.

Even to his mother it was apparent—
when the blue-aproned nurse came into the
northeast end of the maternity ward
bearing his squeals and plump bottom
looped up in a scant receiving blanket,
bending, to pass the bundle carefully
into the waiting mother-hands—that this
was no cute little ugliness, no sly baby waywardness
that was going to inch away
as would baby fat, baby curl, and
baby spot-rash. The pendulous lip, the
branching ears, the eyes so wide and wild,
the vague unvibrant brown of the skin,
and, most disturbing, the great head.
These components of That Look bespoke
the sure fibre. The deep grain.

His father could not bear the sight of him.
His mother high-piled her pretty dyed hair and
put him among her hairpins and sweethearts,
dance slippers, torn paper roses.
He was not less than these,
he was not more.

As the little Lincoln grew,
uglily upward and out, he began
to understand that something was
wrong. His little ways of trying
to please his father, the bringing
of matches, the jumping aside at
warning sound of oh-so-large and
rushing stride, the smile that gave
and gave and gave—Unsuccessful!

Even Christmases and Easters were spoiled.
He would be sitting at the
family feasting table, really
delighting in the displays of mashed potatoes
and the rich golden
fat-crust of the ham or the festive
fowl, when he would look up and find
somebody feeling indignant about him.

What a pity what a pity. No love
for one so loving. The little Lincoln
loved Everybody. Ants. The changing
caterpillar. His much-missing mother.
His kindergarten teacher.

His kindergarten teacher—whose
concern for him was composed of one
part sympathy and two parts repulsion.
The others ran up with their little drawings.
He ran up with his.
She
tried to be as pleasant with him as
with others, but it was difficult.
For she was all pretty! all daintiness,
all tiny vanilla, with blue eyes and fluffy
sun-hair. One afternoon she
saw him in the hall looking bleak against
the wall. It was strange because the
bell had long since rung and no other
child was in sight. Pity flooded her.
She buttoned her gloves and suggested
cheerfully that she walk him home. She
started out bravely, holding him by the
hand. But she had not walked far before
she regretted it. The little monkey.
Must everyone look? And clutching her
hand like that. . . . Literally pinching
it. . . .

At seven, the little Lincoln loved
the brother and sister who
moved next door. Handsome. Well-
dressed. Charitable, often, to him. They
enjoyed him because he was
resourceful, made up
games, told stories. But when
their More Acceptable friends came they turned
their handsome backs on him. He
hated himself for his feeling
of well-being when with them despite—
Everything.

He spent much time looking at himself
in mirrors. What could be done?
But there was no
shrinking his head. There was no
binding his ears.

"Don't touch me!" cried the little
fairy-like being in the playground.

Her name was Nerissa. The many
children were playing tag, but when
he caught her, she recoiled, jerked free
and ran. It was like all the
rainbow that ever was, going off
forever, all, all the sparklings in
the sunset west.

One day, while he was yet seven,
a thing happened. In the down-town movies
with his mother a white
man in the seat beside him whispered
loudly to a companion, and pointed at
the little Linc.
"THERE! That's the kind I've been wanting
to show you! One of the best
examples of the specie. Not like
those diluted Negroes you see so much of on
the streets these days, but the
real thing.

Black, ugly, and odd. You
can see the savagery. The blunt
blankness. That is the real
thing."

His mother—her hair had never looked so
red around the dark brown
velvet of her face—jumped up,
shrieked "Go to—" She did not finish.
She yanked to his feet the little
Lincoln, who was sitting there
staring in fascination at his assessor. At the author of his
new idea.

All the way home he was happy. Of course,
he had not liked the word
"ugly."
But, after all, should he not
be used to that by now? What had
struck him, among words and meanings
he could little understand, was the phrase
"the real thing."
He didn't know quite why,
but he liked that.
He liked that very much.

When he was hurt, too much
stared at—
too much
left alone—he
thought about that. He told himself
"After all, I'm
the real thing."

It comforted him.

YOUNG HEROES—I

TO KEORAPETSE KGOSITSILE (WILLIE)

He is very busy with his looking.
To look, he knows, is to involve
subject and suppliant.
He looks at life—
moves life into his hands—
saying
Art is life worked with: is life
wheedled, or whelmed:
assessed:
clandestine, but evoked.

Look! Look to this page!
A horror here
walks toward you in working clothes.
Willie sees
hellishness among the half-men.
He sees
lenient dignity. He
sees pretty flowers under blood.

He teaches dolls and dynamite.
Because he knows
there is a scientific thinning of our ranks.
Not merely Medgar Malcolm Martin and Black Panthers,
but Susie. Cecil Williams. Azzie Jane.
He teaches
strategy and the straight aim;
Black volume;
might of mind, Black flare—
volcanoing merit, Black
herohood.

Black total.
        He is no kitten Traveler
and no poor Knower of himself.

        Blackness
is a going to essences and to unifyings.
"MY NAME IS AFRIKA!"
            Well, every fella's a Foreign Country.

This Foreign Country speaks to You.

YOUNG HEROES—II

TO DON AT SALAAM

I like to see you lean back in your chair
so far you have to fall but do not—
your arms back, your fine hands
in your print pockets.

Beautiful. Impudent.
Ready for life.
A tied storm.

I like to see you wearing your boy smile
whose tribute is for two of us or three.

Sometimes in life
things seem to be moving
and they are not
and they are not
there.
You are there.

Your voice is the listened-for music.
Your act is the consolidation.

I like to see you living in the world.

YOUNG HEROES — III

WALTER BRADFORD

Just As You Think You're "Better Now"
Something Comes To The Door.
It's a Wilderness, Walter.
It's a Whirlpool or Whipper.

THEN you have to revise the messages;
and, pushing through roars
    of the Last Trombones of seduction,
the deft orchestration,
settle the sick ears to hear and to heed and to hold;
the sick ears a-plenty.

It's Walter-work, Walter.
        Not overmuch for
brick-fitter, brick-MAKER, and wave-
outwitter;
whip-stopper.
Not overmuch for a
Tree-planting Man.

Stay.

YOUNG AFRIKANS

of the **furious**

Who take Today and jerk it out of joint
have made new underpinnings and a Head.

Blacktime is time for chimeful
poemhood
but they decree a
jagged chiming now.

If there are flowers flowers
must come out to the road. Rowdy!—
knowing where wheels and people are,
knowing where whips and screams are,
knowing where deaths are, where the kind kills are.

As for that other kind of kindness,
if there is milk it must be mindful.
The milkofhumankindness must be mindful
as wily wines.
Must be fine fury.
Must be mega, must be main.

Taking Today (to jerk it out of joint)
the hardheroic maim the
leechlike-as-usual who use,
adhere to, carp, and harm.

And they await,
across the Changes and the spiraling dead,
our Black revival, our Black vinegar,
our hands, and our hot blood.

PAUL ROBESON

That time
we all heard it,
cool and clear,
cutting across the hot grit of the day.
The major Voice.
The adult Voice
forgoing Rolling River,
forgoing tearful tale of bale and barge
and other symptoms of an old despond.
Warning, in music-words
devout and large,
that we are each other's
harvest:
we are each other's
business:
we are each other's
magnitude and bond.

SPEECH TO THE YOUNG
SPEECH TO THE PROGRESS-TOWARD
(Among them Nora and Henry III)

Say to them,
say to the down-keepers,
the sun-slappers,
the self-soilers,
the harmony-hushers,
"Even if you are not ready for day
it cannot always be night."
You will be right.
For that is the hard home-run.

Live not for battles won.
Live not for the-end-of-the-song.
Live in the along.

To the Diaspora

MUSIC FOR MARTYRS

Steve Biko, killed in South Afrika
for loving his people

I feel a regret, Steve Biko.
I am sorry, Steve Biko.
    Biko the Emerger
laid low.

Now for the shapely American memorials.
The polished tears.
The timed tempest.
The one-penny poems.
The hollow guitars.
The joke oh jaunty.
The vigorous veal-stuffed voices.
The singings, the white lean lasses with streaming
yellow hair.
Now for the organized nothings.
Now for the weep-words.

Now for the rigid recountings
of your tracts, your triumphs, your tribulations.

A WELCOME SONG FOR LAINI NZINGA

Born November 24, 1975

Hello, little Sister.
Coming through the rim of the world.
We are here! to meet you and to mold and to maintain you.
With excited eyes we see you.
With welcoming ears we hear the
clean sound of new language.
The language of Laini Nzinga.
We love and we receive you as our own.

TO BLACK WOMEN

Sisters,
where there is cold silence—
no hallelujahs, no hurrahs at all, no handshakes,
no neon red or blue, no smiling faces—
prevail.
Prevail across the editors of the world!
who are obsessed, self-honeying and self-crowned
in the seduced arena.

It has been a
hard trudge, with fainting, bandaging and death.
There have been startling confrontations.
There have been tramplings. Tramplings
of monarchs and of other men.

But there remain large countries in your eyes.
Shrewd sun.
The civil balance.
The listening secrets.

And you create and train your flowers still.

from The Near-Johannesburg Boy and other poems

WHITNEY YOUNG

1921-1971

Whitney, you were
a candid structure hulking in event.
And you confounded and offended them out there.
They saw you,
arch and precise.
They saw that you were wise, arch, and precise.
They did not like it, Whitney.

We
remark your bright survival over death.
We share your long
comprehension that there is exhilaration
in watching something caught
break free.

TORNADO AT TALLADEGA

Who is that bird
reporting the storm?—
after What came through
to do some landscaping.

Certain trees
stick across the road.
They are unimportant now.
They cannot sass anymore.
Not a one of these, the bewildered,
can announce anymore "How fine I am!"
Here, roots, ire, origins exposed,
across this twig-strewn, leaf-strewn road they lie,
mute, and ashamed, and through.

It happened all of a sudden.

Certain women and men and children
come out to stare.

THE NEAR-JOHANNESBURG BOY

In South Africa the Black
children ask each other:
"Have you been detained yet?
How many times have you been
detained?"

The herein boy does not live
in Johannesburg. He is not
allowed to live there. Perhaps
he lives in Soweto.

My way is from woe to wonder.
A Black boy near Johannesburg, hot
in the Hot Time.

Those people
do not like Black among the colors.
They do not like our
calling our country ours.
They say our country is not ours.

Those people.
Visiting the world as I visit the world.
Those people.
Their bleach is puckered and cruel.

It is work to speak of my Father. My Father.
His body was whole till they Stopped it.
Suddenly.
With a short shot.
But, before that, physically tall and among us,
he died every day. Every moment.
My Father . . . .
First was the crumpling.
No. First was the Fist-and-the-Fury.
Last was the crumpling. It is
a little used rag that is Under, it is not,
it is not my Father gone down.

About my Mother. My Mother
was this loud laugher
below the sunshine, below the starlight at festival.
My Mother is still this loud laugher!
Still moving straight in the Getting-It-Done (as she names
it.)
Oh a strong eye is my Mother.
Except when it seems we are lax in our looking.

Well, enough of slump, enough of Old Story.
Like a clean spear of fire
I am moving. I am not still. I am ready
to be ready.
I shall flail
in the Hot Time.

Tonight I walk with
a hundred of playmates to where
the hurt Black of our skin is forbidden.
There, in the dark that is our dark, there,

a-pulse across earth that is our earth, there,
there exulting, there Exactly, there redeeming, there
    Roaring Up
(oh my Father)
we shall forge with the Fist-and-the-Fury:
we shall flail in the Hot Time:
we shall
we shall

THE GOOD MAN

For Haki.
In the time of detachment,
in the time of cold.

The good man.
He is still enhancer, renouncer.
In the time of detachment,
in the time of the vivid heathen and affectionate evil,
in the time of oral
grave grave legalities of hate—all real
walks our prime registered reproach and seal.
Our successful moral.
The good man.

Watches our bogus roses, our rank wreath, our
love's unreliable cement, the gray
jubilees of our demondom.
Coherent
Counsel! Good man.
Require of us our terribly excluded blue.
Constrain, repair a ripped, revolted land.
Put hand in hand land over.
Reprove
the abler droughts and manias of the day
and a felicity entreat.

Love.
Complete
your pledges, reinforce your aides, renew
stance, testament.

Force our poor sense into your logics, lend
superlatives and prudence: to extend
our judgment—through the terse and diesel day;
to
singe, smite, beguile our own bewilderments away.
Teach barterers the money of your star.
In the time of detachment, in the time of cold, in this time
tutor our difficult sunlight.
Rouse our rhyme.

INFIRM

Everybody here
is infirm.
Everybody here is infirm.
Oh. Mend me. Mend me. Lord.

Today I
say to them
say to them
say to them, Lord:
look! I am beautiful, beautiful with
my wing that is wounded
my eye that is bonded
or my ear not funded
or my walk all a-wobble.
I'm enough to be beautiful.

You are
beautiful too.